'Marriage is o

Lauren said it we
hitting her head ag

Riccardo raised his dark winged eyebrows and
spoke coldly. 'This is beginning to sound like
one of your English pantomimes—I say you
will, you say you won't. I shall make the choice
easier for you. You will marry me or, I assure
you, Rebecca will be mine and you will never
see her again.'

Dear Reader

Spring is just around the corner; for some this new season may bring a dose of 'spring-fever'—perhaps starting a new diet, thinking about a holiday, or cleaning your house from top to bottom. Others will welcome the longer, lighter days and the first flowers. Whatever your mood, this month Mills & Boon has a great selection of bright, fresh romances, with tempting backgrounds: Greece, Africa, Taiwan and the spectacular Winter Carnival in Venice to name but a few... and we're planning plenty more in the year to come!

The Editor

Catherine O'Connor was born and has lived all her life in Manchester, where she is a happily married woman with five demanding children, a neurotic cat, an untrainable dog and a rabbit. She spends most of her time either writing or planning her next story, and without the support and encouragement of her long-suffering husband this would be impossible. Though her heroes are always wonderfully handsome and incredibly rich, she still prefers her own loving husband.

Recent titles by the same author:

CIRCLES OF DECEIT
DANGEROUS DOWRY

YESTERDAY'S PASSION

BY

CATHERINE O'CONNOR

MILLS & BOON LIMITED
ETON HOUSE   18-24 PARADISE ROAD
RICHMOND   SURREY   TW9 1SR

*First published in Great Britain 1993
by Mills & Boon Limited*

© Catherine O'Connor 1993

*Australian copyright 1993
Philippine copyright 1993
This edition 1993*

ISBN 0 263 77934 3

*Set in Times Roman 10 on 12 pt.
01-9303-55794 C*

Made and printed in Great Britain

CHAPTER ONE

LAUREN snatched up the phone, pushing her blonde hair from her face in agitation. She had been waiting for this call, for some explanation. Mitchell had only told her that the company manager was very taken by Beccy's stunning looks and longed to meet the child's mother. It seemed rather odd to Lauren, but he had promised to ring her the moment the photographic session finished. She had been against the idea from the start, not wanting her daughter to get involved with modelling while she was still so young. She wanted her to keep her innocence for as long as she could.

She answered abruptly, 'Yes.'

Lauren's stomach sank suddenly as she clutched the phone tightly until her knuckles turned white. Her face drained of all colour as she heard the familiar chilling tone.

'I have your daughter.' He paused then said hoarsely, his bitterness adding menace to his voice, 'Or should I say our daughter?'

Lauren froze, her pale blue eyes staring in disbelief at the phone; her whole body was immobile as the icy chill of bitter memories swept over her.

'Riccardo,' she managed to whisper through her thin white lips as she tried to swallow the lump of fear in her throat.

'Yes, Riccardo,' he replied quietly, his accent more pronounced as he struggled with his own emotions. Lauren was shaking so much that she leant on the table for support; her legs were failing under her and she was unable to speak as her mouth grew dry at his confirmation. Lauren pressed her damp fingers hard into her forehead as she tried to collect her thoughts, and her stomach clenched in fear as she thought of what he might do. Perhaps even take Beccy out of the country—she had read about such cases in the papers. The thought made her feel sick; she could feel the room spinning.

'Riccardo,' she began anxiously, the underlying fear apparent in her voice, 'I want my daughter back.' She tried to sound cool, calm, in control, but failed on all three counts.

'*Our* daughter,' he corrected her quickly, and she could imagine the flash of light that pierced his midnight eyes as he spat out the words at her.

Lauren moistened her lips; the silence stretched between them for a long time, then she said thickly, 'What makes you think she's yours?' and she heard the sudden intake of breath and closed her eyes, to shut out his painful reply.

'Well, how many bastard children have you had?' he snarled, his voice low and angry. Lauren regretted her words the moment they were spoken. He had called her bluff and now indignation and hostility replaced her initial fear.

'You weren't too sure of your responsibility ten years ago. What's changed?' she demanded, her usual confidence returning.

'Because today I saw her,' he said fiercely, his voice vibrating down the phone. 'You cannot deny it, you know she's mine.' Lauren could hear the possession in his voice, the hurt and outrage.

'I never denied it,' she bit back viciously, '*you* did.' She heard him mumble a curse in his native tongue and smiled bitterly; it was good to hurt him as he had so cruelly hurt her. She felt calmer now, more in control; she was no longer the gauche little student, travelling round Italy drunk on its beauty. The innocence and delight of those days were long gone; she had grown up— had to, she mused silently as she thought of all he had taken from her.

'I want her back, Riccardo, now.' Her voice was stronger, more resolute; she was fighting for her daughter, and determined to win.

'You have had her for so long, and I have only just met her. I wish her to stay with me,' he replied, his voice cold, as if he were issuing a statement for the Press. Lauren clutched the phone even tighter; she knew him too well, understood the unspoken threat in what he said.

'Please, Riccardo, don't do this to me, don't do it to Beccy—she's a child.' She knew she was shouting; she could hear her voice rushing through her head, pounding against her brain. She was close to tears, tears of anger, pain and fear, and her voice trembled with emotion. '*Please*, Riccardo.' She hated pleading with him, hated herself for being subject to him again, yet for Beccy she would do anything.

'I want to see you. I want to talk,' he stated briefly, and Lauren froze, her heart thudding painfully against her chest, her pulse leaping; she had thought about it so often—seeing him again. She had memorised a little speech, which she longed to deliver, telling him exactly what she thought about him. She had changed; she knew that she had wanted to surprise him, to show him that despite everything she had coped, she was now successful, worldly, not the little innocent he had known and betrayed.

Yet she still felt raw; the pain was etched too deep ever to be forgotten or forgiven. She swallowed the rising lump of bitterness as the memories flooded back. He had robbed her of so much—the gaiety and freedom others had enjoyed, *she* had been denied, forced to accept the role of single parent in a hostile world. Now she wasn't sure; there was no point in meeting—it was past, gone, everything between them had died long ago.

'Lauren.' He whispered her name with a gentle caress and she knew why she couldn't meet him. She still couldn't trust herself even after all these years; the sound of her name on his lips caused a whirl of butterflies within her weakened frame.

'Lawyers,' she snapped, resenting the way he made her feel. 'Let's do any talking through lawyers.'

'No, that is not the family's way,' he ground out fiercely. 'This is personal, between you and me.'

Lauren stiffened at the mention of family—*his* family—and she felt her characteristic vulnerability.

'Family, family—when will you learn I'm not interested in you or your family? Just give me back my daughter,' she demanded. He didn't answer and for a moment she thought he had gone, and panicked.

'Riccardo, Riccardo,' she screamed down the phone, her mind racing as fear gripped her throat.

'Yes,' he answered coolly, waiting for her to speak.

Lauren was desperate. 'I'm sorry,' she said quietly. 'I know how much your family means to you.' How she hated him, his slick cleverness; he knew what he was putting her through, and, knowing him, he probably enjoyed it, she thought angrily. 'Beccy is *my* family—you understand that, don't you?' she tried to reason with him, hoping he would weaken—family to him was everything.

'There can be no family without a father,' he retorted brusquely, and Lauren felt a chilling dread come over her. She would have been happier without a father. She did not consider them to be an essential part of family life. Yet she knew exactly what he meant, and she felt sick at the implication of his words.

'Where's Beccy?' she asked, suddenly realising the photo session must be over and wondering what he had done with her.

'She is here, at my offices; I have explained we are old friends and that you shall be meeting us for dinner. Do you wish to speak with her?' he said.

'Yes,' Lauren replied quietly as the sense of defeat swept over her. There was a click as the call was put on another line. 'Beccy—Beccy, darling, you're all right? Yes, of course, as soon as I can,' she reassured her daughter as tears began to course down her face. She was so afraid, yet she knew Riccardo would do her no harm. The call was cut short by Riccardo as if to torment her, and Lauren felt her bitterness and anger grow. She hated him with every inch of her body, with a depth of feeling that frightened her. She wanted to make him pay, after all the pain and humiliation she had suffered, yet he seemed still to be the one in control, and it rankled.

'You see, she is fine—I wouldn't hurt my own child as you have done. I shall send a car for you—be ready in ten minutes,' he said grimly, leaving Lauren no time to protest at his accusation. The telephone line had suddenly gone dead.

Lauren replaced the receiver and stared out of the window at the surging rush-hour traffic below. Rain had begun to fall, heavy and grey. 'Damn him!' she cried bitterly, leaning on the cold window to cool her hot brow.

She had not seen Riccardo for ten years but she had never managed to erase him from her memory. Her own daughter was a beautiful replica of him save for the sheet of wheaten hair she had inherited from her mother. It was those looks that had led her back to her father, and Lauren cursed her own weakness. She had not wanted her to model, but Mitchell had insisted.

Lauren frowned; it was all her fault—she allowed Mitchell to take over so many times as it was easier. She couldn't bear the hurt look on his face, and he had helped her so much. He had explained that it was a one-off photography session for ice-cream, but there was never any mention of the company. Had Lauren taken more notice she would have immediately been alerted by the name Valdi.

She bit her bottom lip in frustration; she had no one to blame but herself. It was all her fault, but she couldn't have prevented her daughter, because once Beccy knew Lydon Carr was to star she was determined to win her mother over. Lydon Carr was the latest teen sensation; it was every girl's dream to meet him. Lauren had reluctantly agreed, telling Beccy this was not the start of a career; now she wished she hadn't. Everything had changed, and fear curled up inside her stomach as her mind raced with possibilities. It was pointless to deny it; she had never rid herself of the ghost of Riccardo— he haunted her every day, and she despised herself, because despite the new life she had he was still there, like a shadow casting a darkness upon her.

They had met when she was young and malleable, seeking the security and love she had never known. She finally thought she was loved and the idea made her giddy with excitement. She was naturally drawn to him; he was so much older in so many ways, and she willingly allowed herself to be moulded by him, bending to his every desire, giving herself freely.

It had been wonderful for a time, the joy of first love, the heady excitement, the sheer thrill of at last being wanted, but the floating on air came to an abrupt end and Lauren had found herself free-falling through the sky with no safety net. The reality she had had to face was unbearable, and Riccardo's attitude was unbelievable. Lauren could remember it all; every last detail was fixed firmly in her mind, every word, every gesture.

She moved from the window and sank wearily into a chair, her mind slowly drifting back to that fateful day. The vivid details were etched on to her brain with desperate clarity. It was yet another incident in her sorry little life. She felt she should be immune to rejection by now, yet he had tricked her so cleverly, making her believe not only in herself but in him. Lauren shook her head; maybe in life you got what you deserved, she thought sadly, her mind travelling back in time.

She stared till her eyes ached at the blue line that confirmed what she had instinctively known for days: she was pregnant! She had been quite sure that Riccardo would stand by her—at ten years her senior he was ready for marriage; but was she? The doubt went over and over in her mind. What did she know of family life, of building a home? And she knew Riccardo would want that, expect that.

She hadn't seen him since they had argued, always the same argument—his precious family. She knew they didn't like her, this English girl of no breeding. They distrusted her pale complexion, her weak blue eyes; she lacked the fire and vitality that was expected of Riccardo's girl. He didn't realise how it tormented her.

She should have been honest in the first place, but she couldn't have stood his pity—and he would have pitied her.

She had been taken into care at the age of seven. Her parents had married young because of the pregnancy. It was doomed to failure and it was little Lauren who suffered the most. Her father felt trapped in a loveless marriage and his violence soon turned on the person responsible. Though the physical scars were healed long ago, Lauren was still scarred deep within. She was frightened of marriage, of commitment, and the thought of family life terrified her. She had no family, no one— even her foster placements had broken down, so as a member of a family she considered herself a failure.

Yet Riccardo spoke of his own mother and father, sister, brothers, aunts, uncles and cousins till Lauren was in a daze—so she conveniently made herself up a family. A respectable English family: mother, father, one brother. Riccardo accepted her scenario, only thinking it strange that she never discussed them in detail, but he insisted that his family would more than make up for that, and it was a thought that did not please her. Their passionate natures frightened her, their closeness she found claustrophobic.

It was six weeks since she had seen him, and she had thought about him daily, longing for him to get in touch.

It had all been so different at first. She had trembled at his touch and her heart had beat tenfold. The sexual arousal he was causing had been quite new to Lauren, and she'd found it both exciting and frightening at the same time. She knew she was falling in love—she had never felt like this before. The thought of Riccardo's muscular body taking hold of hers, stroking her, his soft mouth on hers, made her quiver with delight. She had known they would become lovers; she'd longed for him.

'You're like a breath of spring, so young, so fresh,' he had told her. Lauren grimaced at the memory; how eager she had been to please him! She was an unsophisticated girl—hardly the type this handsome Italian would be interested in. Yet they had spent time together, and then there was a strange sexual electricity between them, and finally he had told her of his desires, warning her of their age difference. She had thought she understood him, thought he felt the same as her.

Lauren's mouth twisted into a bitter smile as she recalled their lovemaking. He had kissed her, a slow, demanding kiss. She had drowned in her own response to him, lost beneath the incessant rhythm of his mouth, which tormented her. At last they had drawn apart, Lauren heady and breathless, and that night she had willingly slept with him, giving herself with an abandon that even now made her blush.

Yet when she had awoken the following day she'd been afraid. She had had no experience and, though he was gentle and kind, even rocking her to sleep in his arms afterwards, she'd felt she had been a disappointment. He had reassured her that everything was beautiful, that he enjoyed her innocence, loved her gentle shyness.

Lauren ground her teeth in anger as she recalled his words; she knew now it had all been a lie, a pretence, and she wondered how many other poor fools had been a victim of his charms. She was a holiday pastime with him. She had been disgusted to find out that she was one of the many virgins he had seduced in the long hot summer vacation. The pain of that reality had hurt her deeply, but she needed his help now.

She walked to the family villa with a heavy heart; they never really welcomed her, but she knew she had to face them. The whitewashed villa, Casa Valdi, was perched up high overlooking Florence, the Baptistry dominating the familiar landscape of red Tuscan tiled roofs. She had lifted her hand to the bell-rope but the door was pulled open before she had a chance to ring.

He had watched her approach, followed her every step up over the hills. She froze. He stood before her, his dark midnight eyes betraying no emotion. She had privately been hoping for a smile of pleasure or at the very least surprise, but she was disappointed. He seemed cold and remote. Lauren's heart leapt at the sight of him. He was dressed in evening clothes, ready for the off, and her visit was an unwelcome intrusion, she thought. The jet-black suit hugged his broad shoulders and firm hips. His dark classical features gave him an air of superiority and his ebony hair glistened with navy highlights. He was the epitome of an elegant, wealthy man, and Lauren felt so unsophisticated in his presence. Yet she had seen another side of him, happy in jeans and T-shirt sitting on the steps of the Medici gallery, sipping ice-cold drinks, completely at ease on the streets with the students. Now he looked equally at ease as the successful heir to a family corporation.

She looked up at him, taking in his size; he seemed much taller tonight, his height almost intimidating. She met his wintry gaze unflinchingly.

'Can I come in?' she asked, hoping her voice was not betraying the turmoil she felt inside. He lifted his dark eyebrows in a mock gesture of surprise, but made no move to step back. For a moment a cold dread came over her; maybe he was going to refuse, to turn her away without even listening.

He allowed himself to study her for a moment longer; she was slim and small, as pale as the moon and her hair like a sheet of ripened corn, long, and swaying in the breeze. Lauren suffered his cold appraisal without a word; she was hurt by his coolness. He seemed aloof, uncaring, and she suddenly began to question the wisdom of her decision. He stepped back a pace, allowing her room to enter; he gave her a mocking smile, his teeth flashing brilliantly against his olive skin.

'Come in.' It was a curt order that contained no welcome, but if she was honest, what could she expect? She had very ungraciously turned him out, refusing to see him or to listen to him after what Maria had told her.

'I've something to tell...' The words dried on her soft lips, her heart skidding to an abrupt halt. Maria was here. It was not surprising—she was practically part of the family, always around. She stood in the large tiled hall, immaculate as ever, her dark eyes watching them both with an intensity that Lauren found alarming. The chic linen suit she wore fitted her to perfection, giving her lithe body a fluidity that was both graceful and sensual.

She was impossible for Lauren to contend with; she glanced down at her pale faded jeans and plain white blouse, and cast a quick look at Riccardo. She felt at a disadvantage and wished she had worn a dress, but the simple blue cotton sundress she owned was hardly much better when faced with such competition.

'You have?' he demanded, and Lauren caught the savage look in Maria's eyes.

'Yes,' she answered flatly; she still wasn't sure how to tell him. She didn't know why she had come—help? Advice? Reassurance? He seemed to offer nothing, not even a welcome. She glared at him, feeling total despair when she saw that his eyes were cold and lacked compassion.

'I'm pregnant,' she blurted out, ideas of delicacy abandoned under his critical eye. She heard Maria take a sharp intake of breath, her face stony grey as she looked at Lauren with contempt. Riccardo said nothing; he remained completely unmoved by the announcement. Maria broke the deadlock—otherwise they all would have remained frozen in that tableau.

'I'm going; if you need me . . . ?' she offered, kissing him lightly on the cheek and flashing a look of anger at Lauren.

He nodded grimly but said nothing, his eyes still fixed on Lauren, as his mind raced. Once the door closed he spoke.

'I need a drink,' he said, walking into the large lounge, to a glass-topped table with rows of different bottles arranged on it. 'Do you want one?' he offered as he glanced back at her.

She nodded. 'Just juice, thanks.'

He poured himself a drink and knocked it back in one then poured himself another as he offered her a glass of orange.

He waited till they were both seated before he spoke.

'Are you quite sure?' he asked, as if speaking to a child. Lauren frowned; even now, while she was carrying his child, he still saw her as no more than a child herself. She lacked all the polish and grace that Maria had, and it hurt.

'Sure? Of course I'm sure——' she began, but his hard voice interrupted with a question that seared her heart.

'Is the child mine?' His grim gaze swept over her, pausing slightly as he saw her slim flat waist soon to be swelling with an inner life.

Her eyes flared with emotion and she gave a gasp. 'How can you ask that?'

The trauma in her voice made him regret his words, but he had to know the truth; she had lied to him before—he knew that now.

'I have to know; it was only the once . . .' he said.

'That's all it takes.'

She was feeling bitter now; there was no rejoicing in the news, just a flat denial, an accusation. They stared at each other, the hostility building between them.

'You want money for an abortion,' he snarled suddenly, jumping to his feet, 'that's why you're here.' His temper was evident in every tense muscle in his body, his eyes flashed with dangerous light and his features took on a sudden harshness that frightened Lauren. She shrank back away from him, her soft blue eyes widening with fear, her wheaten hair falling over the chair in a blaze of yellow.

'No, never! I won't have an abortion,' she screamed out, the very thought chilling her blood; she drew an instinctive hand over her stomach. Then she witnessed what she thought would be impossible. His expression grew even fiercer, his body taut.

'Did I say I wanted you to have an abortion?' he demanded coldly, the distaste in his voice sending a *frisson* of fear down her spine.

She shook her head, unable to answer him, unable to look at his accusing eyes.

'Well, you must have decided something,' he said simply, waiting for her to explain. She swallowed nervously and picked at imaginary bits on her jeans as she struggled to find the right words.

'I'm going to have my baby and bring it up myself,' she said, not raising her head; the effort to remain calm was paramount, and with Riccardo towering over her she was finding it increasingly difficult. She refused to cry, to weaken, but it was growing harder by the minute.

'And where do I fit into these plans?' he snapped, puzzled by her attitude.

She flashed him a quick look; his grim expression was strangely at odds with his melancholy tone. 'I want to go back to England. I need the money, and you could support your child financially...' she said.

'No.'

'No?' she repeated in disbelief; surely he wasn't going to deny he was the father? Refuse them help? Lauren's stomach sank at his words. 'But it's your baby,' she said softly, ignoring the hard ruthlessness of his face.

'How can you be so sure it is my child? I haven't seen you in weeks.' He stopped as he saw the stricken look on her face, her eyes slowly filling. 'Still, if need be I'll marry you,' he continued calmly, looking at her intently till she could stand his steely gaze no longer. She dropped her eyes and pressed her fingers into the palm of her hand till her nails caused her pain.

'Do you love me?' she asked in a hoarse whisper; the quiet plea in her tone was apparent and she looked up at him, anxiously awaiting his reply. It was a cry from her very soul, deep and yearning.

Riccardo hesitated for a moment, causing a sharp pain to sear through Lauren. His eyes darted to the door. Obviously he found the question too discomfiting, she thought miserably as the cold realisation struck her.

'Maria?' he called, and she entered the room, almost apologetic.

'I forgot my bag—sorry,' she said sheepishly as she sauntered over and retrieved it from the chair. Riccardo's eyes never left her for a moment, and Lauren's heart smashed as she was forced to acknowledge that the possibility of his loving her was ridiculous. Maria was much more his type—voluptuous and every inch an Italian.

'I won't marry you,' Lauren confessed softly. She had experienced that at first hand. No child of hers would suffer as she had done. How long would it be before he would say, 'I had to marry you'? And if, like her, the child heard that accusation... She shuddered as she recalled her parents' bitter rows and how she felt responsible because she was the reason for their marriage.

'I'm sorry I came,' she said, rising slightly from the chair.

'Sit down,' he barked, strangely angered by her refusal. 'I shall make the arrangements immediately; we shall marry,' he said grimly, the finality in his voice frightening her. It sounded more like a threat than a proposal. Lauren shook her head.

'I don't want to marry you—you don't have to marry me,' she said quickly before he had a chance to formulate any further plans.

'Damn you, I will marry you!' he roared at her, and she shrank further away. He was pushing her again; she felt trapped; she couldn't cope with all this. His sense of duty, though admirable, was not enough; she wanted his love. There had been a time when she thought she had it, but now she knew the truth. She was just one of many young girls he swept off their feet with his handsome Italian looks, and she wasn't prepared to force a man into a loveless marriage.

'No, I am not going to marry you just because of the baby. I'll go now—we never have to see each other again,' she informed him with as much coolness as she could muster, although she felt her heart shatter. He had spoken not one word of love, yet she remembered times when the word was forever on his lips.

'Don't threaten me, Lauren, I don't like it,' he said, his voice dangerously quiet. 'If you are carrying my child then I shall marry you; I will not have a bastard,' he spat vehemently at her.

She knew it was pointless to argue so she nodded in silent agreement, despising herself for her weakness, yet his fierce temper frightened her.

She feigned tiredness later and returned to the little inn where she was staying. She jumped when she heard the knock on the door, frightened in case Riccardo caught her in the act of packing. To her relief it was Maria.

'Lauren,' she began huskily, drawing her into her arms, 'I am so sorry, so very sorry. I tried to warn you, to tell you so many times that you were a plaything,' she said softly.

Lauren swallowed the rising lump in her throat and confessed as tears began to fall. 'I know you did, Maria, and I thank you for that, but he had me fooled. I thought he really loved me.' She sniffed as she began throwing clothes into her case.

'He is a master at it; as you know, I am one of the family—even Riccardo looks on me as a sister. I see this year in, year out—it is his way,' she explained, a sadness in her voice. Lauren carried on packing, the words echoing in her mind and thudding out a death-knell.

'I've been such a fool,' Lauren cried, collapsing in a heap on the bed and sobbing loudly. She was broken-hearted; all the dreams she had had were gone. She felt so hopeless, so alone.

'Don't cry. Waste no tears on him; think of yourself, your child. Here, please take this,' Maria said softly, patting her back. Lauren looked up and stared in wonder at the small bundle of notes being offered to her.

'I can't. I could never pay you back,' she gasped, amazed at Maria's generosity and tempted to take the much needed money.

'You must,' she insisted, pressing the money into her hand. 'It is the least I can offer. Perhaps if I had told you earlier of his reputation . . .' She shrugged expressively. 'Now,' she sighed, 'it is too late, but take this and go. If you return to England now he will never find you. If you stay you will be forced into marriage, but he will not be faithful to you and you would suffer even more pain.'

Maria squeezed her hand and left.

Lauren packed immediately and made her way to the main foyer. With the money from Maria she would be able to fly home. She decided to go straight to the airport to put as much distance as she could between herself and Riccardo. She paid her bill and sat waiting for the taxi— and froze in disbelief as she saw Riccardo march through the entrance, his anger apparent in every stride.

Lauren shrank back, hoping to conceal herself, but his razor-sharp vision spotted her cowering figure. His dark eyes flashed immediately to the scruffy case at her feet then his eyes darted back to her face.

'I thought you would try something like this,' he growled, snatching her arm in a vice-like grip. 'I thought it might be better if you stayed at the family home,' he informed her crisply, pulling her to her feet with ease.

Lauren struggled fruitlessly for her freedom and cried breathlessly, 'Let go, Riccardo. I'm going home.'

'Home for my wife and child is here,' he snapped back, drawing her to the hotel entrance. Lauren caught sight of her taxi, her route to escape, and she pulled herself free.

'I'm not your wife and this child isn't yours either,' she cried. 'I tried to trick you merely for money but someone else paid me off so you're off the hook,' she sneered, making a bolt for the car. Riccardo followed, blocking the car door; his eyes had narrowed and his jaw was tight and firm.

'The child is not mine?' he demanded, his voice so cold that it froze her heart. The pain in her chest was threatening to choke her, but she knew this was her only chance.

'No,' she spat with venom. 'Thank God, the child is not yours.' She pushed him aside and dived into the taxi.

She never looked back, never saw the stunned expression on his face as she drove away. She would bring up this child alone rather than marry Riccardo Valdi. She would love and treasure this child, she would give her all she could; she knew she would never have the wealth and power of the Valdi family, but she would have love.

Lauren's eyes filled with fresh tears as she recalled Maria's kindness. She had understood Lauren's feelings and sympathised with her problem. She had kindly given her the money to return to England—a kind gesture that Lauren never forgot. She had so much to thank Maria for, and she now felt a stab of regret that she had never been able to return the favour.

Lauren sighed as she stood up and began to pace the room; she was not looking forward to meeting Riccardo. She bit softly into her lower lip.

She had tried so hard over the last ten years to put the past behind her. She had slowly built a new life for herself, and though it could never match the lifestyle Riccardo had offered her she was content enough. She worked in an agency, having started out as the receptionist. She had had ambitions of being a teacher, but now all her personal ambitions were put on one side while she had a young child to provide for; her only concern was to earn a salary. She had never made a real effort to gain promotion—she lacked confidence—but she had slowly climbed up the ladder so that she was now personal assistant to the managing director—his 'right hand' as he jokingly called her; but she knew herself that she was indispensable. Every promotion had given her not only a little extra money but also the confidence she so badly needed.

Over the years she had grown from a skinny young girl into a shapely, attractive woman. She still had her long golden hair, but once she had given birth to Beccy her figure had developed and she worked hard at a dance class to maintain her figure. She owned an attractive property, small but big enough for her and Beccy, she was well travelled—she had everything, she thought grimly, except peace of mind. Try as she might to erase the past, she had always known that she and Riccardo would meet again.

She shuddered at the thought; she was not looking forward to this confrontation. Yet she was stronger now, she had grown up—the birth of the child she was forced to support alone had seen to that, she thought bitterly. Lauren's mind was in a turmoil. She had always told

Beccy that her father had died—what if Riccardo told her the truth?

She gave an involuntary shudder; the shock could be very damaging if not handled correctly, thought Lauren anxiously. Then she shook her head. Perhaps she need never know—what possible good could come of it now? Beccy was best left with her dream that her parents, though very much in love, were separated by death. If Riccardo was expecting to win her round with his charm, or force her to an agreement with his veiled threats, then he was wrong, she decided as the ringing of the doorbell broke into her thoughts. She opened the door to a smartly dressed chauffeur.

'Mr Valdi sent me, miss.' He gave her a dignified nod as he spoke, and escorted her down to the waiting car. It was exactly what she had expected—sleek and expensive, the windows tinted in a smoky grey to afford that extra privacy. Lauren could sense the eager curiosity such an expensive car was generating in the small suburban road where she lived. She felt a flush of colour rush into her cheeks when the driver opened the door and gave a slight nod as she got in.

The drive to his office seemed to take no time at all, and Lauren was anxious. She certainly didn't want Beccy to know the truth, but she already had to admit that might be exactly what Riccardo wanted.

The underground car park was deserted, the cold grey walls rose like a prison around her, and she walked with the same slow, pensive steps to the lift as would a man facing his executioner. The doors opened on a wide corridor, the floor of which was covered in a thick deep blue carpet, and Lauren felt her feet sink into its deep pile as if she were in damp sand.

Riccardo was waiting in the doorway. Lauren paused, taking a steadying breath; then her heart stopped. He was still as daunting, maybe even more so.

He leaned on the door-jamb, his body lithe and excitingly still. He gave her a long, penetrating look, his eyes piercing her very soul. She returned his look, met his gaze head-on without showing the fear she was feeling inside. Antagonism, blazing and strong, surged through Lauren's mind. The depth of the emotion shocked her, and she closed her eyes to shut out his hard visage. She could feel his eyes burning into her, the intensity of his hatred apparent in his cruel expression.

'You're more beautiful than I remember, Lauren.' There was a flicker of admiration in his dark eyes as they slid over her shapely body, lingering on her long, slim legs.

Lauren stiffened at that, her mouth tight and compressed. She swept past him, entering his office without even acknowledging his presence. He followed her, and Lauren froze as she heard the door crash to a sudden close. She swung round to face him, trying to suffocate the mounting fear she was feeling. She was more angry, though, and saw no reason to hide it.

Riccardo studied her for a few minutes, his body still, the lithe, well-muscled contours of it dressed impeccably in a dark business suit, his white shirt open at the neck, revealing a few stray dark hairs. She had never seen him look so furious, his ebony eyes fixed on her with an expression she preferred not to analyse, but she shivered when she saw it and suddenly became aware of how isolated she was.

The room was silent and empty, and Lauren's eyes darted quickly round the impressive office. The furniture was large, masculine, and she noticed to her dismay that Beccy wasn't here.

She felt her stomach tighten in fear; was she already too late? Had he taken her away? She had always known he would, if ever he found her. She recalled his family, their terrible pride in their ancestry; Beccy had too much of his dark Latin look to be rejected as she herself had been.

'Where's Beccy?' she snapped, her blue eyes glittering, as she confronted Riccardo's black anger.

CHAPTER TWO

THERE was a moment of silence as Riccardo and Lauren glared at one another, then he spoke.

'In the staff canteen, having a milkshake in the company of my secretary. I thought it best we talk alone first,' he told her icily, and Lauren was grateful that Beccy was not here to witness their confrontation.

'What do you want, Riccardo?' she asked, not wanting to play his cat-and-mouse game, distrusting herself with every passing minute. He was too male, his whole sexuality so overpowering that it was impossible to deny that he affected her. He raised his dark winged eyebrows expressively, his face turning white under his tanned skin.

'You bitch—you know what I want.' He stared at her with hate flashing from his eyes. Lauren stood her ground; she knew he would be angry, and she couldn't honestly blame him—it must have been a terrible shock suddenly to see himself mirrored in miniature. She swallowed nervously.

'You can't have her, so let's not waste each other's time.'

His fist slammed down hard on the desk, the sudden noise making her jump.

'Straight down to business, eh?' he mocked, his eyes sliding over her body, making a slow inventory of her every contour. 'You're quite the businesswoman, aren't you?' There was a cruel mockery to his voice that made Lauren hate him even more.

'That's right—I came only because you have my daughter,' she replied.

'Mine too!' he roared, pointing at her with an accusing finger. 'The child is mine, a Valdi—she bears our stamp.' His eyes gleamed with a passion she had not expected.

Lauren spoke quietly but calmly in an effort to make her point clear and to defuse the electric atmosphere that was developing.

'She has inherited some of your looks, but the resemblance to you and your family ends there—— Thank God,' she added under her breath.

Yet he had heard her—she knew that from his swift reaction. He grabbed at her wrists, his fingers sharp and angry, but she deftly flicked her hands and released them, and stepped back. For a moment he was stunned, and looked at her in amazement.

'Motherhood has certainly taught you some tricks.' He gave a quiet laugh, a flash of—was it admiration on his face? she wondered as she still watched him closely.

'A single female with a child is an easy target. I had to make sure I could defend myself,' she explained simply. He looked at her thoughtfully.

'And Rebecca—who protects her?' he asked.

'Don't underestimate her; she too is trained—she had a junior black belt in judo before she was nine,' Lauren told him with pride.

His eyebrows rose in approval and surprise. 'Hardly a feminine pastime for a girl,' he said coolly.

'But you don't know her, do you?' It was a cruel, unnecessary jab, but Lauren couldn't help it. How dared he criticise how she brought up Beccy?

His eyes darkened at her words, his jaw tightening. 'Well, I'm here now and want to make amends,' he said.

Lauren gave a cold, hollow laugh. 'How very touching,' she said mockingly, flicking her hair back impatiently.

He smiled when he saw her action; despite her cool façade he recognised the gesture. Whenever she was under pressure she would flick her hair.

'Don't push me, Lauren,' he warned her, his voice as sharp as flint with impatience, hating the person she had become, hard and sharp.

'Where's Beccy? I want to see her,' she demanded, not trusting him for a moment.

'I've told you,' he began, then his eyes darkened as realisation struck home. 'You think I may take her, deny her her mother as you have denied her to me,' he bit out suddenly, his eyes flashing warning lights, forcing her to silence. 'I think that would be a drastic measure—I do not wish to be forced to take such action,' he said quietly, the threat in his voice sending a chill through Lauren.

She glanced at him uncertainly; he was as handsome as ever—even the years had been good to him. He hadn't changed; the sparse grey hairs that touched his temples only seemed to add to his distinguished features.

Lauren shivered as she understood the trouble she was in. Now he knew for certain that Beccy was his daughter, he wanted her.

'I'm sorry,' she began, hating herself for jumping to the wrong conclusions; but he certainly had not ruled out the possibility—that was obvious.

He cut in dismissively, 'Our daughter is a credit to you; she is a very lovely child—not just physically, you understand, but she is ...'

Lauren jumped in at his pause, disliking the fact that he was referring to Beccy as 'our' daughter instead of hers.

'She's mine, always has been. You have no right to come here upsetting everyone,' she shouted out, angry at his acceptance of this unreal situation.

'I have every right,' he growled, stepping closer towards her; but Lauren held her ground, tossing her head back in a defiant gesture. He mumbled as he turned away, 'You've changed.'

Lauren gave a hollow laugh. 'Ten years, it's a long time; what did you expect—the same silly, innocent girl?'

He turned back to face her; she still looked as fragile, as innocent, but he could sense the core of steel she had developed.

'What went between us is past, but there is Rebecca,' he told her, his cold voice freezing her heart.

Beccy, Beccy, a voice cried within her; she was annoyed that he was already taking over, changing her name. She didn't want him, not anything to do with him, yet his saying that what had gone between them was past gave her a sudden stab of pain.

'Beccy? What's Beccy go to do with you?' she demanded.

'I'm her father, I want to help,' he said.

'You're certain now that she is yours, are you?' she mocked. 'I think you're ten years too late with your concern,' she added bitterly, sinking into a chair, her emotion spent.

He bent his head, admitting the justice of her words. 'But I wasn't given a chance, was I? Not a real chance,' he bit back at her, the contempt in his eyes clearly visible. Lauren felt a stab of guilt momentarily, but she could justify her actions whereas he could not.

'I gave you a chance—I needed your help then, but not now,' she retorted angrily, wondering why she felt the need to defend her actions.

'I suppose Mitchell gives you all the help you need,' he snarled, and Lauren paled.

'How do you know...?' she whispered, remembering the antagonism between the two before.

'Rebecca is far more forthcoming than her mother ever was,' he informed her, enjoying the stunned expression on her face. 'Do you sleep with him?'

The audacity and offensiveness of the question infuriated her. What right did he have to ask such questions? Lauren resisted the desire to slap his hard, handsome face, fearing the consequences of such an action.

'What is it to do with you?' she demanded angrily.

'I was willing to marry you ten years ago, and I still am,' he said briefly, allowing the impact of his words to sink in.

Lauren's head shot up in disbelief. She stared at him in amazement and then gave a cruel laugh when she saw just how serious he was. She jumped to her feet, her eyes flashing.

'What makes you think I'd marry you? I certainly didn't want to ten years ago, and nothing has changed,' she shouted, angry at his suggestion.

He looked stunned for a moment; but what did he expect? Gratitude? Pleasure at his ridiculous proposal? she thought angrily as she studied him. His eyes darkened momentarily, his mouth hardening to a grim line. Every feature on his ruthless face held a menace that frightened her. He stepped closer, a malicious grin forming on his face. He placed his hands gently but firmly on Lauren's shoulders, and she could feel the

hidden strength in his fingers, see the unleashed violence
in his expression.

'You don't frighten me,' she snapped, aware that her
eyes were widening and her knees growing weak.

'Good; a wife should love her husband, not fear him,
and believe me, Lauren, you will be my wife,' he said,
his mouth twisting into a sardonic smile.

Lauren stared at him in disbelief; she wanted to laugh
but the determined look on his face soon stopped her.
She shook herself free from his angry grip and moved
away, surveying him slowly with a critical eye, her contempt evident in her expression.

He stood perfectly still, allowing her appraisal without
uttering a sound, his equilibrium not shaken in the least.
When her eyes finally reached his face she was met by
his dark eyes laughing at her. Lauren steeled herself not
to blush, and thankfully succeeded. Her pale blue eyes
flashed vividly at him.

'I'm sorry, I shall have to turn down your gracious
proposal,' she said sarcastically. He frowned, a muscle
throbbing in his temple.

'You're not married, are you?' he demanded suddenly, as if the thought that she might be had never oc-
curred to him.

For a moment Lauren was tempted to lie—it would
have been so easy, yet even though ten years had passed
she had never quite recovered from loving Riccardo, and
every man paled in comparison. She tried to read his
expression, but it was impossible.

'Are you?' he snapped, and Lauren allowed herself a
smile.

'Is that so hard for you to imagine? As you say, a
family for Beccy would need to include a father.'

She saw a flicker of emotion in his eyes as his poker expression fell for a moment. He stepped closer, and Lauren caught the familiar aroma of his pungent after-shave. He gripped tightly at her forearms, pinning her into immobility, his strong fingers biting into her soft skin. Lauren flinched as he drew her closer till his warm breath caressed her cheek.

'It cannot be true,' he whispered hoarsely, his eyes diamond-bright, searing her soul as he stared at her.

Lauren swallowed nervously, already aware of his proximity; she tried to fortify herself against the feelings he was arousing in her. Her whole body was coming alive, tense with anticipation. She began to tremble as she felt her own defences beginning to weaken and slowly crumble.

'Tell me, is it Mitchell?' he demanded again irritably, as he could bear her silence no longer.

'No,' she mumbled, shaking her head softly. 'No, I've never married.'

He gave her a triumphant smile and his teeth gleamed as he broke into silent laughter, yet he did not release her. 'That's because you still love me—yes?' His arro-gance amazed her and his perceptiveness hurt.

'No, I never married, because few men will take on another's child. You didn't want to be her father yet you robbed her of the chance of ever having one,' she spat at him through clenched teeth. How she hated him, she thought bitterly, her eyes viewing him with cold disdain. He hadn't changed, still as aloof and superior as he had always been, still playing the role of a stud, imagining she compared all men to him.

Lauren's heart leapt as the words 'Don't you?' silently jeered, echoing in her mind, with such a ring of truth that it was hard to completely deny them. Riccardo's lips curled back from his white teeth in a savage snarl.

'My God, you have changed,' he muttered. 'I never thought I'd ever hear you say anything like that. Whatever happened to you?'

Suddenly she was very still, staring at him with renewed anger; despite the antagonistic way he spoke, the cold menace in his voice, she was not afraid of him. The pent-up anger, bitterness and pain of being alone spilt out with all the venom she had.

'*You* happened—you took away my innocence, my naïveté, my trust in others. I would have been left nothing, but I had Beccy, and I'll see you in hell before you'll take her from me.' Her voice crackled with animosity, the full depth of her feeling apparent by her sparkling eyes and flush of colour.

'I have every right to see my child,' he insisted.

'I think you forfeited yours,' she snapped back.

'Forfeited it? How the hell could I do that? You ran out on me, left me. Let's not forget that,' he stormed bitterly, sinking his hands deep into his trouser pockets as he paced the room. Lauren felt a rush of colour to her face as the truth of his words hit her.

'Why, Lauren, just tell me why?' he snarled, his eyes glittering with fury.

For a moment Lauren did not know what to say—it all seemed so long ago; but then she had been so much younger. Too young to cope with the demands Riccardo's family would have made.

'You didn't love me,' was her simple reply—the only thing she could think of saying when faced with such anger and distrust.

His eyes narrowed to diamond chips, as he viewed her, allowing her words to slowly sink in. 'That doesn't mean I couldn't love my child—want to love my child.'

Lauren couldn't help but notice that he made no mention of her, and for some reason, even though she had lived with that knowledge for so many years, it still hurt her.

'I'm sorry—I thought by now you would be married, have your own children . . .' she tried to explain, but his anger erupted again.

'Well, I'm not married and I don't have children and the only child I have you have kept from me, you little bitch,' he said grimly. 'Don't you think I had a right to know?'

'You might have taken her,' she cried, her eyes widening with fear as she remembered he still might.

'Probably—I can offer so much more,' he retorted, his reply making her immediately on her guard.

'You would take Beccy from me?' she asked, a plea in her voice.

He studied her coldly for a few moments, then turned his back to her and cursed himself silently for seeing the pain in her eyes.

'That would hurt you,' he said softly, 'but you care nothing for *my* pain—she is my daughter.'

He kept talking about *his* daughter, as if he had to keep reminding her. Lauren was filled with dread at his quiet confession; she noted his slumped shoulders and saw for the first time a vulnerability in him. She longed to reach out to touch him; she had never felt more at one with him than at this moment. They were sharing the love they both had for Beccy yet the pain of the past was still with them, preventing her from moving.

'You don't have to worry—I'll not prevent you from seeing Beccy, not now,' she said quietly. He swung round, his head tossed back, and he gave a laugh of derision.

'What overwhelming generosity! After ten long years you are finally to allow me visiting rights,' he scoffed.

'I think that's only fair...' she began.

'Fair?' he jeered. 'Now what would you know about that?'

'What more could you hope for?' she retorted, not wanting to fight or threaten, but she knew she was being forced into a corner.

'Now I see that familiar naïveté again. What type of lawyer could you afford, and, as for judges, who would not award sole custody to the Valdi family rather than a single parent with dubious morals?' he mocked.

'That's a lie,' she whispered back hoarsely, doubt already growing in her mind.

'Is it? I hear Mitchell often calls, forcing my daughter to model.' He tutted and shook his head. 'It doesn't sound too good to me.'

'You bastard!' she shouted, knowing that if custody was fought he would win.

'That's right, and believe me I will be if you force me to fight for Rebecca,' he threatened.

It was at this moment the door opened, and Riccardo's secretary stuck her head around the door, noting the electric atmosphere with an apologetic nod.

'I'm sorry—just thought I'd let you know we're back, Mr Valdi.' She disappeared again, but Lauren was wasting no time—she began to make for the door, her steps nearly breaking into a run. Riccardo, anticipating her every move, darted in front of the door, effectively blocking her way. He stood with his long legs apart, his arms folded rigidly against his hard chest.

'You're not running out on me again,' he growled, not moving an inch.

Lauren looked up at him, trying to take the measure of the man. He was a fighter, and used to winning, but she couldn't allow him to come into her life again; she had taken so long to recover from the last hurt.

'No, I'm not running out like a frightened rabbit, but I am going—and with my daughter,' she told him coolly, fixing her eyes on him with ice-cold determination, the calm façade completely at odds with the turmoil she felt inside.

He watched her mouth; it was still as soft despite the angry words she spoke. He knew that he could take those trembling lips and gently kiss her into a more submissive mood of acceptance, yet he couldn't do that—not after ten years, not now, with their daughter as part of the jigsaw. He felt a stab of remorse; had he hurt her that much that she had changed so dramatically, or was her cool, hard exterior only a thin veneer?

'My daughter too,' he reminded her with equal bitterness; she had robbed him of so much that he wasn't going to allow her to go and take his daughter again.

'For God's sake, Riccardo, she is a child, a person, not a possession to be argued over. She doesn't even know you,' she informed him angrily, longing to get away, to put as much distance as she could between them.

'And whose fault is that?' he countered bitterly, his dark eyes flashing with sparks of passion, his well-muscled body tensing with a primitive desire to protect his own offspring.

Lauren gave a derisive laugh, to cover her feeling of guilt. It was true—she hadn't allowed him to be a father but, worse than that, she had taken that opportunity of having a father away from Beccy, and that hurt.

'Marry me?' The proposal was halfway between a command and a plea. He took her hand, holding it gently, squeezing it with affection, knowing that his touch would weaken her. He could never forget how they were together—flames of desire consuming both with a passion so intense that finally making love would be a satisfying climax.

Lauren stiffened at his touch, his long tapering fingers wrapped around her hand firmly but tenderly, and she despised her body's betrayal as her pulse leapt. She felt the familiar heat grow in her body at his touch, and tried to draw away—yet he was arousing in her so many forgotten dreams and desires. An awakening began, stirring deep inside, buried and denied for so many years that it hurt to feel them again. He stroked her thumb with slow deliberation across her throbbing pulse and her whole body shivered with anticipation.

'Why?' she managed to ask, looking at him and noting the hazy, slumberous look in his eyes and dropping her gaze immediately in fear that her own response might be as obvious.

'I want you *and* Rebecca,' he said hoarsely as he pulled her closer till she caught the pungent aroma of his aftershave.

'Want? Want?' She drew back; the possessiveness in his voice frightened her. 'We aren't commodities like your stocks and shares. A child needs love, and, let's be honest, you could provide Beccy with everything but that,' she threw back at him as she moved away, her voice cutting and harsh.

He drew a hissing breath, his hands clenched suddenly into fists at his sides. The lean body tightened, a pulse beating rapidly at the base of his throat.

'Just because there is no love between us, it doesn't mean I couldn't love my daughter,' he said hoarsely, and Lauren winced at his words.

'Well, whether you could or not is purely academic, as you're not going to have the opportunity,' she spat out wildly, and she saw the devilish lights in his eyes blaze into an inferno. His jaw gripped tight, his mouth a cruel, thin white line.

'You go too far, Lauren,' he warned her, stepping closer and staring at her for what seemed an eternity. She felt herself move away; his anger was apparent in every muscle of his body. 'I shall have my daughter with or without you,' he threatened quietly, the unleashed violence flaring in his eyes. Lauren couldn't allow him to take her; she wasn't prepared to let her go—Beccy was far too precious to her.

'You'll never have her—do you hear me? Never!' she shouted at him, pushing him away with every morsel of strength she had in her. He hadn't expected that, and for a moment he lost his balance. Lauren made full use of his bewilderment; she raced for the door, and was through it in seconds, snatching Beccy's arm and dragging her with her, leaving his secretary silent and puzzled. Rebecca protested as her mother pulled her from the offices and rushed down the corridor. Panic gripped Lauren as she banged frantically on the lift button; her eyes darted backwards to see if she was being pursued.

'What's wrong, Mum?' demanded Beccy anxiously, looking at the strained expression on her mother's usually calm features. 'Did he make a pass at you?' she persisted, sensing some thing was amiss and enjoying the excitement.

Lauren shook her head and frowned disapprovingly. 'No, no, of course he didn't,' she answered quickly. 'I can't imagine what gave you such an idea,' she continued suddenly, aware of the picture she must have given her daughter. She pulled her hair smooth and took Beccy's hand. 'I'm running late, that's all,' she lied, and Beccy looked at her with the same distrust she had just seen so clearly mirrored in Riccardo's eyes.

The journey down in the lift took forever—Lauren expected it to come to an abrupt stop any time, and she tapped her feet impatiently on the lift floor and listened half-heartedly to news of Rebecca's day. When the lift stopped the doors refused to open; Lauren pressed every button, but to no avail, then the lift slowly began its ascent and Lauren knew she was trapped.

'What's going on, Mum?' persisted Beccy, with the same perceptiveness as her father. Lauren looked down at her and smiled; it was all too complicated for her to understand, and she wanted to protect her from the heartache she had known. She braced herself as the lift came to a halt, whereupon the doors slid silently open and Riccardo immediately stepped in.

'Sorry I was detained, ladies; perhaps now we can go to dinner.' He smiled charmingly, his face alight with pleasure. He made no comment about what had gone on between them yet as Lauren was about to protest, her eyes shining with anger, he fixed his eyes on her, warning her to be silent and, as she did not want Beccy to witness how she felt, she merely lowered her head.

Riccardo leaned casually back against the lift wall, his eyes bright and hungry, looking as his eyes slowly followed the curves of her body. Lauren stiffened at his blatant appraisal, and he gave her a deliciously wicked smile. She felt her insides turn to jelly and she despised her body's betrayal.

'Well, Rebecca, what's your favourite food?' he asked; he sounded genuinely interested, not in the least condescending, and Beccy responded to his adult approach.

'I like hamburgers and pizzas and french fries,' she informed him, a slight blush on her cheeks, and Lauren felt a stab of anger as she realised that even her daughter was not immune to his charm. He lifted his eyebrows in mock horror.

'Hardly a suitable diet for a growing girl,' he said coolly, looking at Lauren for some response, but she ignored his gibe and continued to stare blankly at the floor. She was struggling to build up a defensive wall against him.

'I often go for a pizza or hamburger when Mum's working late,' said Beccy, eager to show just how grown up she was, and Lauren silently groaned as she thought how it would sound in court.

'That's not too often, Beccy, and besides, you never go alone—Mrs Farrell is always there for you,' she reminded her gently, and stared at Riccardo in silent combat. He acknowledged her explanation with a wry smile.

'A Mrs Farrell takes care of Rebecca when you're too busy?' he asked drily, his eyes deep and unfathomable. Lauren bristled at the unspoken criticism.

'Yes, she does, and we are all very happy with the arrangement,' she snapped, aware of the sharpness in her tone. He ignored the fire in her eyes and turned his attention to Beccy, who was watching them both with amused interest.

'And you, Rebecca—does this arrangement suit you?' he asked, lifting her chin gently so that he could see her eyes. Lauren swallowed the rising lump in her throat as Beccy, unaware of her betrayal, answered honestly.

'Mum has to work. I miss her sometimes—like when I'm on the netball team and the other mums are there.'

Lauren turned her face away as hot pin-heads pricked against the backs of her eyes; she bit softly into her lower lip as waves of guilt engulfed her. She was so lost in her own thoughts that she failed to notice that the lift had stopped. Riccardo touched her hand gently and Lauren jumped, her eyes wide with fear, wondering what he was about to say.

'Come on,' he whispered gently, as if aware of her pain. Lauren swallowed and nodded as they walked over to his awaiting car. Beccy was already seated inside, marvelling at the luxury.

'I wish we had a car, then we could go out on drives at weekends, though Mitchell takes us out,' Beccy said as she fiddled with the ashtrays and amused herself flicking the windows up and down. Lauren gave her a disapproving look but she was too excited to notice.

'Mitchell?' asked Riccardo casually, but Lauren was not fooled by his easy tone.

'It's Mummy's boyfriend,' Beccy informed him knowingly; unaware of the dark shadows in his eyes, she continued, 'They are going to get married one day— Mitchell says so.'

'Beccy!' Lauren cried, mortified at this revelation; but it was partly true. Mitchell longed for Lauren to agree, but she knew she would never marry. Still, it would do Riccardo no harm to think she was about to do just that.

'Well, maybe one day soon,' Lauren said coyly, directing a smile at Riccardo which he chose to ignore. Instead he directed his conversation at Beccy.

'Do you like picnics, Rebecca?' asked Riccardo; his voice held a warmth that brought back bitter memories to Lauren. Beccy nodded enthusiastically.

'Yes, one year when I was little we went to Devon, and we went out every day,' she told him, unaware of his wry smile.

Lauren coloured with embarrassment; was he doing this deliberately, letting her know how little Beccy had and what he could offer? She turned to look out of the window and caught his handsome profile as she did so; he was still as attractive as ever, yet there was a menace about him now, an unspoken anger and bitterness she had not seen before—or was too blind to see, she corrected herself briskly.

Riccardo spent the journey talking to Beccy; they seemed completely at ease with one another, like long-lost friends, and Lauren resented it. The car drew up outside a smart Italian restaurant, and the name painted across the windows with an artistic flourish made Lauren stop in her tracks. She stared at the green letters in disbelief. Then she turned and faced Riccardo with blazing eyes.

'Is this your idea of a joke?' she asked angrily, the pain in her chest causing her words to tumble out in a torrent. He raised his eyebrows to allow the glimmer of arrogant amusement to shine from them.

'I thought it would be rather romantic, recapturing forgotten dreams,' he whispered, taking her hand with a gentle but firm control.

'Nightmares would be a more apt description,' she bit back at him, but he merely laughed at her words as he escorted her and Beccy inside.

CHAPTER THREE

THE heady aromas of Italian cooking assailed her nostrils, bringing with their bouquet a mixture of bitter-sweet memories. The rich scents of fresh garlic, pungent oregano and sweet-tasting basil filled the air, and Lauren inhaled deeply, allowing herself to enjoy the tantalising aromas, the very essence of Italy. It was so easy to imagine the hot sunshine and the coarse red wines she had drunk so freely all those years ago.

She cast Riccardo a sideways look; he was watching her, aware of the effect the atmosphere was having, and she wondered what he hoped to achieve by it. Surely he couldn't imagine that reminding her of the past would be an enjoyable experience? she mused as she watched him warily, still not trusting him.

They stood for a moment, staring at each other across the unbridgeable gap of ten long years. She knew how charming he could be, but she also detected in him a ruthlessness she had not seen before, a frightening coldness that she knew could easily turn to anger. He wanted Beccy, and he always got what he wanted. She looked deeply into his eyes, trying to find a glimmer of the man she had known, but she searched in vain. The cold blankness of his eyes made her shudder; she knew he was trying to persuade her to marry him, and she was willing to play along in order to gain time. But he had never been a patient man, and she knew he would tire soon. She had no intention of marrying him—the very idea was ludicrous.

A shiver went down her spine; there was something dangerous about him now, and despite her brave talk he frightened her. She shuddered at the thought of the real battle which they would fight, and her heart went out to Beccy. She would have to know the truth, and Lauren wasn't sure how to approach the subject. She would do anything to prevent her daughter from suffering, but surely a loveless marriage was too much. How long could she and Riccardo maintain the illusion of being happy? It was hopeless.

She was so lost in her thoughts that she hadn't noticed they had been steered to a corner table.

'It's great here, isn't it, Mum? I can't wait to tell Charlie,' Beccy declared.

Riccardo's face was marred with a look of disapproval, and Lauren felt herself smile, noting how already, and with such ease, he seemed to have slipped into the role of a doting father.

'Charlotte, her closest friend,' she supplied, grinning, and Riccardo nodded silently. It was a shared moment, and Lauren felt a sadness that she had never been able to share with him all of Beccy's life.

She allowed herself to look round the interior of the restaurant, and she felt her stomach plummet, and her heart began to thud uncomfortably against her chest as her eyes grew wide in disbelief.

It was exactly like the little café she and Riccardo used go to in Florence. It looked the same, even down to the smallest detail: the posters, the green checked tablecloths, the wax-laden bottles that adorned each table, the candle adding an intimate glow to the surroundings, even the bare brick walls reminded her so much of the little café where she and Riccardo first met.

'You recognise it?' he asked, his voice strangely at odds with his austere expression. He placed his warm hands on hers as he spoke, and Lauren immediately drew back as if she had been scalded. She wanted to deny that such a place held any memories for her, but she knew that was impossible.

Instead she answered softly, 'It was such a long time ago.' She swallowed the rising lump in her throat that was threatening to choke her, and she was grateful for the distraction of a waiter, who proffered her a menu. She bent her head, intent on the array of dishes before her; she had always loved Italian food but rarely had enough money to enjoy dining out. Beccy leant across to her and whispered quietly in her ear, and a smile spread across Lauren's face as she nodded heartily in agreement. Riccardo looked at them both, his eyes flashing.

'What are you two plotting?' he demanded, a grin of amusement lighting his face, and for a moment Lauren saw a flash of the man she had known and loved. Beccy put her fingers to her lips and shook her head at her mother. Lauren laughed at her antic; it was pointless to deny that Beccy used more gestures than was usual, and Lauren was forced to admit that was probably due to her Italian heritage.

When the waiter returned to take the order he looked patiently at one then the other till Lauren gave a smile of encouragement to Beccy. Then, taking a deep breath, Beccy began to order and, though her accent was not flawless, the Italian was perfect. '*Bravo*! *Bravo*!' cried Riccardo in delight, applauding his small daughter with obvious admiration. Lauren too smiled warmly at her and leant across the table, giving her hand a squeeze. The two adults then ordered; Lauren had perfected her accent years ago, but it still came as a surprise to Riccardo. He looked at her in amazement.

'Your Italian has improved greatly since the last time we met; now we can converse in your language or mine and still not understand each other,' he said cryptically.

Lauren shrugged; there was a ring of truth in what he said, yet talk they must—she knew that—or she was in danger of losing Beccy altogether.

'I had no idea you had business connections in England,' Lauren said, trying to keep the conversation on neutral topics.

'I have widened the company's interest over the last few years. I saw that food—any food—had a rapid turnover with little cashflow problems. Young people especially like anything new, different, so, with imaginative packaging and the right image, my new venture should be a success,' he explained, smiling broadly.

Lauren did not return the smile; the Riccardo she knew took no interest in business yet now he seemed to be absorbed in the whole mesh.

'But why England? Why now?' persisted Lauren, wondering who was to blame for his return into her life.

'Lydon Carr—we have made an advert of him for every country he is doing a concert in. He's very popular,' he added knowingly, winking at Beccy.

'So under your direction the company has changed considerably,' mused Lauren, half to herself. Riccardo fixed his dark eyes on her with an intent that unnerved her.

'Yes, I needed something, some challenge, a new venture. Work is a marvellous panacea. It helps one forget,' he informed her, allowing her to make what she wanted of his words.

Lauren dropped her gaze. Was she responsible for this change or had Riccardo simply grown up?

'The company though is still firmly in banking?' she asked, unable to understand his words.

'But of course—but it did not appeal to me. I wanted to make my own way—with help, naturally.' He laughed, acknowledging his family's wealth.

Lauren nodded; she was glad for some reason that he had not settled to the family banking career but had chosen to follow his own instincts. She knew he would be a success—he was that type; he had never known failure.

The meal was delicious; each of them had chosen something different so there was a great deal of sharing. Beccy had ordered *Calamari fritti*; she enjoyed all seafood but this was her favourite. Lauren, because she was feeling quite queasy as the day's events raced around her mind, decided to have the *Pomodori alla Siciliana*— tiny baked stuffed tomatoes served with a crisp green salad. Riccardo's appetite was not in the least affected— he ordered a pasta starter and a main course to follow. He looked a little disappointed when no one wanted anything else.

'I'm sorry, we don't eat that much,' confessed Lauren, shrugging her shoulders and flicking the hair from her face.

'It is too expensive for you to eat well, eh?' he asked sharply, viewing Beccy with concern—and she was certainly eating with unconcealed enjoyment.

'No, not at all; Beccy has her dinner at school, and in the evening we have a light supper by the fire, don't we, Becs?' She tried to make it sound homely so that he would feel guilty about destroying what they had, but instead he nodded thoughtfully and asked Beccy,

'You like these meals at school?'

'They stink,' replied Beccy, squeezing her lemon fiercely over her fish as if the very thought was abhorrent.

Lauren frowned and tutted her disapproval. 'Don't exaggerate, Beccy; you know you quite like them,' she admonished, knowing he was storing all this up to use against her. Beccy raised her head at the sound of her mother's sharp tone and saw the look of apprehension on her face. She was puzzled for a moment then she smiled.

'Yes, they're OK,' she said, her eyes darting from one adult to the other with unconcealed interest. 'Where did you two meet?' she asked, suddenly curious. Lauren felt a rush of colour to her face; she had never lied to Beccy about her origins but she hadn't been entirely honest either.

'We met here,' laughed Riccardo as Beccy's eyes widened in disbelief.

'Here?'

'Well, in the real Firenze,' he admitted, grinning at her. 'That's where I live,' he explained.

'Oh,' said Beccy. 'Did you know my father, then?' she asked in all innocence. Lauren stiffened and stared at her open-mouthed; she began to stand, unable to face the look that she knew would be on Riccardo's face. She felt his strong hand grip her arm as he pulled her firmly back down on to her chair.

'Sit,' he commanded as if speaking to a dog, and Lauren winced at the harsh tone.

'Well, did you?' persisted Beccy, unaware of the two adults' behaviour.

'Your father came from Florence, did he?' Riccardo asked in a smoky voice—ever so polite and interested, fumed Lauren as his grip remained as firm as ever on her arm.

'I'm sure you're not interested in all that, Mr Valdi, and we really must be getting home now,' Lauren interrupted, but her voice began to fade as his grip tightened still further, his strong fingers biting into her soft warm flesh.

'On the contrary, I am fascinated to hear what became of your husband,' he said coldly, his voice quiet and threatening, his eyes blazing with unconcealed anger. 'Do go on,' he urged Beccy, giving her a winning smile she responded to immediately.

'No, Mummy wasn't married to him; they both fell madly in love, but he died before they could marry. Isn't that sad?' she asked Riccardo, and he nodded in agreement.

'Yes, that's sad, very sad,' he answered her hoarsely, and Lauren felt a pang of guilt. She avoided looking at Riccardo; she knew he would be furious yet at the time it seemed the most sensible story to tell Beccy. It was pointless stopping any longer after her revelation, and Lauren was longing to put as much distance as she could between her and Riccardo.

The drive back to her house was conducted in silence; Beccy was sleeping drowsily in the rear of the car and Riccardo had barely spoken since Beccy had told her tale. The atmosphere was strained and Lauren knew he was brooding over what had been said to him. She could sense his unspoken anger; it was clearly etched in every line of his face, his eyes were as black as midnight, yet a fire of temper blazed within them, causing sparks of devilish lights. Lauren felt she was sitting next to a volcano, waiting for the inevitable eruption but unable to prevent it. The rain had begun falling again, and the wipers flicked across the windscreen in hypnotic rhythm.

'Thanks for the meal,' she said suddenly, unable to cope with the ominous silence any longer. For a moment she thought he was going to ignore her, then his head snapped round suddenly and he barked,

'Why, Lauren, why?'

She could hear the pain and outrage in his voice but she had little sympathy for his opinion.

'I had to tell her something. I thought that was for the best,' she faltered. He grimaced at her words, though kept his eyes fixed firmly on the road ahead.

'What was wrong with the truth, Lauren?' he snapped, his voice harsh and guttural. She saw his hands tighten around the steering-wheel till his knuckles turned white.

'The truth? The truth that her father didn't want her or her mother?' She gave a hollow laugh as the bitterness swept over her.

The car came to an abrupt halt, forcing Lauren forward suddenly. He turned to face her and she shrank back at the look of fury on his face. He leant over her, pinning her body in the seat, his own hard, muscular body across hers. She trembled at his touch but he wasn't aware of it; the only emotion he felt was anger.

'The truth, my dear,' he spat at her, tracing a cold finger down her face with icy precision, 'is that you ran out—ran away from her father, ran away from commitment, and made your daughter a——'

'Stop it, stop it!' cried Lauren, struggling to free herself and hating him talking about Beccy like that.

'But that's the truth—the real truth, and I think she deserves to know,' he threatened softly, not moving an inch.

She could smell his familiar aftershave as she tried to move away from him, and she froze. She couldn't possibly tell Beccy—not yet; the shock would be awful. She shook her head in denial, avoiding his steely gaze.

'I can't tell her,' she whispered through thin lips.

'Can't or won't?' he asked. 'She has to know, she has a right to know, and when we are married she will see me as her true father.'

Lauren gasped, her mind reeling; she was immediately alert.

'I've told you, I'm not going to marry you,' she answered him, ignoring the determined look on his face. He lifted his shoulders dismissively.

'I'm not asking you, Lauren, I'm telling you,' he replied quietly. She closed her eyes to shut out his hard, angry face and sighed; the situation was hopeless.

They drove home in an angry silence, the tension increasing by the minute. Lauren's pulses leapt with nervous confusion as he stopped the car and turned to look at Beccy sleeping peacefully. He leant over the back of his seat and stroked a wisp of hair from her face. The gesture was so tender and loving that Lauren felt a surge of pity. The look of love in his eyes was truly genuine and the realisation that he was determined to have his daughter frightened her.

'I'll carry her in.' It was a curt statement, not an offer, and Lauren felt it was easy to oblige. She raced ahead of them, opening the door to her tiny terraced house and flicking on the light. She frowned as she noticed the damp patch creeping further up the wall—today's non-stop rain had made it even worse. There was no way she could disguise it, and the musty smell it gave to the small hall was hardly welcoming. Riccardo paused in the doorway, his height dwarfing the hall still further.

'Take her straight up,' Lauren said calmly, jerking her head at the narrow staircase that led directly from the hall. He nodded, taking the stairs with ease despite the weight he was carrying, and Lauren followed behind.

'This room,' she said, pointing over his shoulder; he tapped the door open with his foot and laid Beccy down gently. His eyes darted round the room and Lauren was grateful that she had recently had it refitted. The wardrobe covered a multitude of builders' nightmares.

'I'll see to her now, thanks. Goodnight,' she said, hoping he would take the hint and leave; but that idea died instantly as he shook his head.

'No, Lauren, we still have things to discuss,' he said icily, in a low, angry voice. He gave her a chilling smile as he turned to go downstairs. 'Don't be too long,' he added as he disappeared, and Lauren felt her heart thud a little faster, her pulse beating furiously at her throat. She sat down on the bed, quite still as she allowed the dilemma she was in sink in. Then she drew a shaky breath; she couldn't marry him, he must realise that, she thought grimly, so the only question to be settled was that of visiting rights.

She shook her head in dismay when she remembered his response last time she had mentioned that. It took some time to settle Beccy—pulling clothes off a sleeping child gently enough so he or she did not wake up was an art which Lauren had perfected. She drew the cover over her daughter and her heart sank. It was like seeing an angel: her olive-toned skin held a glow, her beautifully formed eyebrows swept over her long dark lashes and her hair fell like a golden sheaf over her slim shoulders. She couldn't give her up, and her anger and bitterness increased when she thought he had returned with his mixture of charms and threats to take Beccy from her.

She took a steadying breath as she prepared to face him, and walked down the stairs with tenacity. She pushed the door open and stopped; he had removed his jacket, abandoning it over the chair along with his waistcoat and tie. He had kicked his shoes off and lay relaxing on the sofa, his legs crossed, his eyes fixed on the display of photographs that adorned the wall.

Lauren was not fooled by his calm façade—she could sense his anger. The pictures on the wall only added to his bitter feelings. She had had a photograph taken every birthday; the first one was a small snap of a tiny pink bundle—Beccy a few hours old; the next was of a chubby one-year-old propped up securely and proudly displaying one tiny white tooth—and so they went on, a complete catalogue of her every year. Lauren saw the pain etched on Riccardo's face as he turned and viewed her disdainfully; she felt herself colour under his cold eyes, and her pulses quickened. She swallowed nervously.

'Thief!' he spat bitterly at her. 'You have robbed me of all this,' he said, sweeping his arm out towards the photographs. She shivered, her blood running cold as she thought how he might react.

'I did what I thought best—still think *is* best—for Beccy,' she insisted, turning away from him and bending to light the tiny gas fire.

There was a brief pause during which Lauren felt the tension increase within her. She rested back on her legs; sitting on the floor, next to the fire, she suddenly felt very cold. She sat quite still, waiting for him to speak, and when he did she looked at him in amazement, her eyes wide.

'I think we should marry as soon as possible—a special licence will only take three days to arrange.' A smile curled his mouth as he spoke. She gave him a sharp, irritated glance.

'I've told you, marriage is out of the question,' she said wearily, feeling as if she was hitting her head against a brick wall.

He moved swiftly at these words, his cool fingers encircling her slim wrist as he pulled her to her feet. She looked at him with intense dislike, her body stiffening because of his proximity. They stood close, too close; alarm bells began to ring loudly in Lauren's ears as she struggled to remain calm.

'This is beginning to sound like one of your English pantomimes—I say you will, you say you won't. I shall make the choice easier for you. You will marry me or, I assure you, Rebecca will be mine and you will never see her again.' He spoke slowly, allowing each word to have full impact.

'You can't be serious!' exclaimed Lauren in panic, not really doubting his words for a moment. She searched his face for a glimpse of the man she had known, some tender part that she could appeal to. The search was fruitless, however; he remained cold, aloof, his eyes narrowed as he nodded his head.

'Believe me, Lauren, to doubt me would be foolish in the extreme,' he warned her softly. 'Marriage to me will hardly be an ordeal,' he reminded her arrogantly. Lauren's head shot back her hair, which fell like a golden waterfall over her shoulders, and she felt her temper flare, bringing a brightness to her eyes.

'If I decide to marry you it will be on the strict understanding that it is for Beccy's sake,' she told him coldly.

He raised his dark winged eyebrows in amusement and gave a quiet laugh.

'I hardly think you are in a negotiating position. I trust you mean our marriage is not to include sex?'

Lauren nodded seriously, never taking her eyes from him, watching him very warily. He shrugged.

'I shall consider your suggestion,' he drawled in a smoky voice.

'I mean it, Riccardo, I want nothing to do with you,' she retorted through clenched teeth. Riccardo laughed as he moved closer to her.

'That's strange, because I sense perhaps you do.' His hand slipped to her shoulder, his grip tightening on her wrist as he drew her closer. 'I am not usually wrong about such things,' he said.

Lauren felt the searing impression of his fingers and shivered, avoiding his gaze. 'Leave go,' she said unsteadily, frightened by the emotions he was arousing in her.

Riccardo studied her intently. 'Now why should I do that? You might run away again,' he murmured, his narrowed gaze sharp as he raised his hand to stroke her face. 'I always knew you would grow into a real beauty, Lauren,' he said, his voice becoming deeper and more husky. Her gaze met his with a start.

'I think it best if you go,' she said shakily as she saw the hungry look in his deep, sensual eyes. The impact sent volts of excitement through her. He smiled, his eyes lazy and slumberous.

'Soon,' he drawled, pulling her softly towards him. She watched his dark head approach with increasing alarm. He seemed to move in slow motion, every move carefully co-ordinated. Her heartbeat increased to terrifying proportions, her pulse thudding quickly in her throat as he drew nearer with tantalising slowness. Lauren felt her eyes droop, her lids closing as she automatically tilted her head back to meet his.

His mouth fastened on hers with remarkable tenderness; it was easier to wash away the last ten years as he coaxed her to respond. Her pulses leapt with confusion as she allowed his long fingers to slide down her back, pulling her still closer to him till she could feel his hard, muscular chest pressing against her. Her lips parted willingly and the kiss deepened, warm and firm. She kissed him back with a passion that surprised her. She ran her fingers through his dark hair, pulling him closer to her, her mind dizzy with emotion. Riccardo drew back slowly, his eyes glittering.

'See? I was right,' he said drily.

Lauren's eyes shot open to be greeted by the triumphant smile on his face. Her body slowly iced over as the full meaning of his words sank in. Her body had betrayed her. She stared at him, her face rigid and pale.

'You bastard!' she breathed through tight lips. 'Why are you doing this?' she asked, totally perplexed. He seemed to be playing some bizarre game with her, with rules only he knew and understood. Riccardo smiled without warmth.

'It is to show you that you have no power, you will be mine on my conditions.' He pulled her roughly into his arms, holding her with a cruel hardness. Then he released her, almost pushing her from his arms; she raised her hand to slap him, to rid his face of that superior smile. But he was faster, his hand gripping hers before she even reached his cheek. She stared at him in frustrated anger while he smiled down on her angry upturned face.

'I see you have a lot to learn,' he drawled menacingly, his eyes roaming over her with a cool detachment. 'I shall of course enjoy teaching you.' His hands went to her shoulders as he reached for her to pull her back into his arms, but she resisted. She pushed him away desperately.

'Don't you dare touch me again,' she snapped angrily, and her eyes flashed a warning as she took up a defensive posture. Riccardo laughed, but his face was still hostile.

'I'm really frightened,' he drawled, his voice and expression full of amusement.

'Beccy will never forgive you if you hurt me,' she flung breathlessly at him, warding him off with both her hands pressed firmly on to his hard chest, just managing to hold him at arm's length, her face scared and anxious. Riccardo raised one dark brow.

'She will understand a great deal more when we are married,' he said with a cold smile as he ran his finger down her cheek to her soft lips. 'Children learn about relationships through what they see and hear.'

Lauren gasped as she remembered what she had learnt, and she knew with a cold certainty she was not going to subject Beccy to that. 'I've told you, I haven't decided to marry you,' she said tightly. Riccardo laughed under his breath, his mouth slowly parting to reveal his strong white teeth.

'So you did,' he mocked lazily, 'but for some reason I just don't believe you.'

Lauren stared at him, her body rigid with complete shock. She saw the expression in his eyes and her breath caught in her throat as she realised he was paying her no attention. Her cheeks blazed with colour, her anger so intense that she could hardly move.

'You're not listening—I shan't marry you...ever!' she shouted as her hand flew to his cheek. The sudden, unexpected impact caused his head to snap back, a deep red mark colouring his cheek. He took her shoulders in a fierce grip, pulling her towards him. He viewed her slowly, and she watched him, his eyes flashing with fury, pleased at last that he had finally understood how she felt.

'It is you who refuses to listen; I want my daughter—she will be mine. You, however, I'm beginning to have my doubts about.' His strong arms pulled her even closer to him and she struggled fruitlessly against his overpowering strength. She beat his back with as much vigour as she could, but it made no difference. His mouth sought hers and he forced a kiss on her lips that held only bitter anger and resentment. She tried to twist away, her body writhing against his, but Riccardo was stronger and she was unable to escape. Finally he pulled back, leaving Lauren breathless, her face flushed.

'Maybe you would be some use as a wife,' he mocked, as he slipped his feet back into his shoes.

'Get out of here!' she spat through her teeth as she flung his jacket and tie at him. He caught them deftly and grinned.

'Is that any way to talk to your future husband?' he laughed as he left the house.

Lauren slammed the door behind him as hot tears threatened to flow. She sighed, her mind racing while she made sure the house was secure before going up to bed. She felt weak and tired; she went through the motions of brushing her hair but the usual brisk strokes were missing. Then she climbed wearily into bed. The sheets were cool and crisp and she lay awake for a long time, staring into the blackness of the night.

Thoughts of Riccardo filled her mind; in spite of everything she couldn't forget how much he had once meant to her. After years of pain and rejection, he had made her feel loved, and his refusal to accept her and their child cut into her heart so deeply, reopening all the other wounds she had suffered as a child.

She closed her eyes, trying to force some sleep, but she was too tense—the day's events turned over and over in her mind. She longed for a good night's sleep, but even when she finally drifted off her dreams were troubled. The tormenting image of Riccardo pervaded her mind, and time and time again she was running away from him; but he pursued her relentlessly, stretching out to snatch Beccy from her arms.

She could feel her heart thudding against her ribs, she could hear his voice calling her back repeatedly. She ran faster, but he was still in pursuit and gaining all the time. She would turn and see his forceful image, his strong muscular legs striding towards her. She tried to run faster but he was getting closer all the time. She ran on, and a pair of heavy ornate doors flew open; she ran in, then stopped in horror. She could see his features quite clearly now, his raven-black hair thick and unruly, tossed with the exertion of running. She looked down at her clothes; she was wearing a wedding dress, and as he slipped the ring on he grasped Beccy's arm and they both disappeared.

Lauren gave a cry of anguish as she sat upright in bed. She was bathed in sweat, her body burning and shaking with fear. She shut her eyes tightly and with a cry of despair turned on to her side and wept bitterly into her soft pillow.

CHAPTER FOUR

THE morning light pierced through the closed bedroom curtains, casting its warm yellow glow across the room. Lauren moaned as she tried to raise her head. It felt like a ton weight; her neck was stiff and her head was throbbing with a dull, incessant pain. She pressed her fingers deeply against her temples, rubbing them fiercely to relieve the tension. She lay still, allowing the pain to sweep over her; it dulled her mind, preventing her from thinking about anything else. She sighed as she stroked her hand across the back of her neck, pulling her hair up and placing it like a golden mantle across her pillow.

At least it was the weekend, and she had no need to be up, yet she knew that to stay in bed would probably only increase the pain. She made her way to the bathroom and smiled as she heard the sound of familiar children's programmes drift uptairs. At least Beccy seemed unperturbed by last night's events.

She clipped up her hair in a loose bunch as she stepped under the shower—and gave out a yell of disapproval as the barely warm water splashed on to her back, startling her. She remembered how she had forgotten to turn on the heater, and laid the blame at Riccardo's door—he seemed to be responsible for a lot of misfortune in her life. The shower was over quickly as the water chilled still further. She wrapped herself up in her towelling gown and made her way downstairs. A noisy cartoon was screaming across the television screen and seemed to race right through Lauren's head.

'Turn that down,' she snapped at Beccy as the pain increased. Beccy darted to the screen and switched off the set.

'I'm not that bothered—I shan't watch it,' she said, a sulky look spoiling her face.

Lauren sighed. 'There's no need to play the martyr— I just wanted a bit of peace. It was on too loud and I've a banging head,' explained Lauren, correcting her daughter unwillingly. Beccy gave an exaggerated sigh and flung herself down on to the chair.

'I'm bored,' she announced with deliberation, waiting for her mother's reaction. But Lauren was in no mood for this; her head ached, and the constant threat of Riccardo hung over her.

'Are you?' she snapped. 'Then why not take that cereal bowl that you've used out into the kitchen and then busy yourself tidying that pigsty you call your room?' she said as she marched into the kitchen and began to hunt for some aspirin.

'They're on the second shelf,' Beccy offered as she placed her cereal bowl in the sink and then carefully filled a tumbler of water for her mother. She passed it to her, their eyes met, and simultaneously they gave each other a sympathetic smile.

'If this headache goes and your room is tidy perhaps we will go to the park this afternoon,' Lauren said kindly, hating any friction between them. She tossed her head back and grimaced as she swallowed the tablets, aware that Beccy was watching her.

'Perhaps you drank too much last night,' Beccy stated, watching her mother with interest. Lauren frowned; she was grateful that Riccardo wasn't here, otherwise he would be able to accuse her of being an alcoholic. He had already put her into the 'neglecting mother' box.

She frowned; he lived in a happy home—what did he know of the harsher realities of life? She had returned to England penniless and pregnant. She had had to give up her chance of studying for a teaching degree and find a more suitable course—one that would teach her a skill quickly. She'd needed to have money for a home for her child.

'No,' she answered Beccy, forcing herself back to to-day's realities. 'I didn't drink that much. I never do,' she emphasised. 'It's probably due to over-work,' she lied, but she caught the doubtful look in her daughter's eyes.

'I like him—I think he's really gorgeous,' Beccy said.

'Who?' asked Lauren, expecting it was yet another teen star. Beccy seemed to fall in and out of love with commendable ease, mused Lauren, waiting for the name of her latest idol.

'Riccardo Valdi,' she answered in amusement.

It was like a body-blow to the pit of Lauren's stomach. She felt a deathly chill come over her. It was unbe-lievable that only twenty-four hours ago her little girl was hers, totally hers, and yet now Riccardo's presence was creeping back into her life, taking over.

She swallowed the pain; she was used to hiding her feelings—years in care had taught her to.

'Yes, he is a...' She paused, unable to find a suitable adjective. She could think of plenty, but none suitable for her daughter's ears. 'He's a busy man—I don't suppose we'll see him again.' Lauren tried to sound casual and unperturbed, but she knew Riccardo too well; he would be back, and the thought frightened her.

'He promised to take me on a picnic,' stated Beccy, proudly confident that he would keep his promise.

'Really?' sighed Lauren, disliking the sound of admiration in her young daughter's voice. 'Go and do your room, darling,' she encouraged with a smile, longing to finish the conversation. Beccy was far too astute for her age; it was only natural with her being an only child, but Lauren could not trust herself where Riccardo was concerned, and she did not want her daughter to have any suspicions. She made herself a coffee and sauntered back upstairs. Her headache was on the wane and the thought of going to the park seemed very attractive as the sun grew warmer.

'Get the door, Becs, I'm just dressing,' she called as she struggled into a figure-hugging T-shirt. She pulled on her jeans and rushed downstairs as she heard a male voice.

'Is that you, Mitchell?' she called as she snatched up a pair of clean socks from the laundry basket. Mitchell called round most weekends, and on such a pleasant day he was bound to want to take them out. The idea suddenly appealed to Lauren. She longed for his uncomplicated view of life, his simple generosity. She wished she could feel something more for him, but she didn't, try as she might. Yet Mitchell was patient and felt sure one day soon Lauren would weaken and decide to marry him—he had offered often enough.

She opened the door still hopping on one leg as she tried to get her sock on—then froze when she saw who the male visitor was, her eyes dilating in fear as her mind raced with the possible reasons for his visit. He was dressed casually in snugly fitting grey trousers that drew attention to his taut, lean body. The immaculate white polo shirt clung to his chest, emphasising the warm tones of his olive skin.

'Sorry to disappoint you—it's not Mitchell,' taunted Riccardo, his mouth hardened, but otherwise he betrayed little emotion as his cool eyes wandered over her body. Lauren allowed herself the luxury of looking as disappointed as she felt. She sank on to a chair with a weary resignation.

'What do you want?' she asked, trying to keep the bitterness from her voice and avoiding the glittering black contempt that was ever-present in his eyes.

'To take us on a picnic,' Beccy squealed with delight, jumping in the air with pleasure. Lauren stiffened and threw an angry glance at Riccardo. She saw a flash of white teeth but there was no humour in his eyes.

'No, we can't go,' she snapped, hating to see the disappointment on Beccy's face. 'We're going out,' she added in a conciliatory tone.

'Yes, but only to the park. Let's go with Mr Valdi—he's brought a hamper and everything,' enthused Beccy, the plea in her voice tormenting Lauren.

'Please, Lauren?' Riccardo asked; his velvet voice held a warmth she did not expect, and her eyes shot up to look at him. Nervously she scanned his face, looking for a trace of the man she had known and loved. She was disappointed; his expression revealed nothing, his dark eyes as deep and as unreadable as the ocean depths. Lauren turned to look at Beccy.

'Aw, please, Mum,' she begged. 'I'll do my room—honest,' she added as an extra incentive.

Lauren sighed. She knew when she was beaten, and knew Beccy would never forgive her if she refused.

'All right,' she agreed without enthusiasm. 'But you do your room first,' she insisted as Beccy rushed for the door. She watched Riccardo's eyes as he followed his daughter's action. For a fleeting moment she felt a pang

of regret; maybe she had been wrong to deprive him of
his child. He turned back suddenly, and she was shaken
by the look of anger on his face.

'Have you told her yet?' he demanded, though it was
obvious by his stance that he already knew the answer.
His dark eyes were glittering with the fire of unspent
emotion, and she saw the tension etched on his ruthless,
carved face.

'Told her what?' asked Lauren shakily, ignoring the
building fury in his eyes.

'You know damn well. She has been without a father
for too long—I want her to know,' he snapped back
grimly, losing his patience.

'I think that's my decision,' she corrected him. She
saw the cold anger on his face, but was determined not
to be afraid. 'I can't tell her,' she added with deep conviction. To tell her the truth now would mean admitting
she had lied, and the whole truth would have to be
known. Lauren did not want Beccy to feel that pain.

'Can't, or won't?' he growled, a hint of menace in his
voice. 'It's no use, Lauren, I mean for her to know. I
want to be a real father for her.' Lauren flinched at the
contempt in his eyes, which was matched by her own.

'Do you? Well, maybe you should stop thinking about
what you want and think about her,' she retaliated
fiercely, her head tilted in angry defiance as she met his
hostility head-on.

'I am,' he snapped. 'I can give her so much.'

'Material wealth,' spat Lauren through clenched teeth.

'Well, there's damn little of it here,' he sneered, his
eyes quickly taking in the small room, which was fur-
nished pleasantly enough but hardly up to his standards.

Lauren felt a hot spear of anger fuel her tiny frame with indignation. How dared he criticise her and the lack of possessions?

'There's more to being a parent than showering children with material goods,' she almost shouted back, the hurt, angry defiance bright in her pale blue eyes. 'It was me who bore her alone in that hospital. It was me who took her for her vaccinations, stayed up with her through the night when she was ill, worried about her on her first day at school, consoled her when she wasn't invited to parties. Me, me, me!' she said, stabbing her finger angrily at herself as the pain and rage of all that responsibility borne alone spilled out. Her eyes filled with unshed tears as she faced him.

'I could have been there,' he stated coldly. 'I would have held your hand while you gave birth, stayed with her when she was ill, taken her to school and given her birthday parties that would have ensured she would have been invited everywhere.'

His voice was strangely soft, almost wistful, but his face remained as cold and ruthless as ever.

'But you—you denied me all that, and now you're trying to place the guilt at my door. Well, try again, Lauren, because the only person around here who should feel guilty is you,' he reminded her with a cruelty that only increased her pain.

The hardness of his voice confirmed her thoughts that there was nothing left between them—only bitterness and hate, and Lauren wanted to shield Beccy from that more than anything. The gulf between them seemed to be widening all the time; the only bond they had was Beccy, and Lauren wasn't prepared to lose her.

'I gave her all my love,' Lauren stated simply, her voice quiet, the admission like a confession. She kept her head lowered, unaware that Riccardo had drawn closer. He took her gently in his arms.

'I have love to give her too. She is my daughter,' he whispered tenderly, his warm breath caressing her face. The anger was suddenly dispelled as Lauren reluctantly nodded. She swallowed the painful hard lump that appeared to be growing in her throat, causing her chest to ache.

'I know,' she admitted, still disliking the possessive tone in his voice yet forced to concede that he too had rights. 'I don't want to lose her,' she said, the anxious tone in her voice softening his attitude a little.

'You don't have to—we will be a family,' he said with such determination that Lauren stiffened. She drew back, frowning, her pale eyes troubled. She didn't want that— could he not understand? She shook her head dully but was unwilling to argue the point. Her aching head had returned with a vengeance, no doubt caused by the flurry of emotions.

'I'll get my coat,' she informed him coldly. 'You seem to have taken care of everything else,' she added—the venom in her voice afforded him some amusement, she knew, and his eyes gleamed.

'Yes, I've taken charge of everything,' he replied; there was an underlying threat in his tone that perturbed Lauren. She pulled her blue windcheater on, zipping it up firmly as a thin barrier against the sheer masculinity of the man. She hated herself for it, but it was pointless to deny he still aroused her more than any man she had ever known.

Within moments they were all sitting in his car, gentle music playing on his stereo, filling the vehicle with a surprisingly relaxed atmosphere. Beccy chatted freely, supplying Riccardo with an inventory of her life. Lauren

sat in quiet solitude, casting covert glances at Riccardo
to see his reaction. He seemed completely at ease, yet
occasionally his mouth would tighten and Lauren felt a
stab of remorse that she had taken Beccy away from
him. She tried to rid her mind of such thoughts; she had
done what was right, she insisted to herself, but a niggling doubt was ever-present. She tried to rationalise her
decision, but it all seemed so long ago and somehow no
longer relevant.

The car ate up the inner-city streets with amazing speed
and comfort, and before long they were cruising in the
open countryside. Lauren sighed; it was so beautiful and
peaceful, the road before them curled like a lazy snake
weaving its path through the undulating green hills,
stilling her troubled soul.

The sun was high in the sky by the time they stopped
to eat. Beccy gave a cry of delight; she loved animals,
birds especially, and he had chosen a wildfowl sanctuary
as their picnic place.

'I thought you'd like animals; I always did when I was
small, and just recently I gave up some of my land to
encourage wildlife—birds, little mammals,' he said,
laughing with unconcealed pleasure at his decision. Beccy
scampered from the car, calling back to Riccardo to
hurry as he drew the hamper from the rear of the car.
Lauren climbed from the car almost reluctantly, in the
sure knowledge that in spite of everything Beccy was
going to remember this day for the rest of her life.

'Take heart, you may enjoy yourself,' teased Riccardo
lightly as he locked up the car. Lauren knew it would
be petty to spoil the day, and she gave him a wan smile
as she followed him with a heavy heart.

The sanctuary was beautiful; it contained a large reception area with bookstalls crowded with animal lit-

erature. There was a small café and a tiny gift shop which Beccy immediately spotted.

'Look at this—isn't he cute?' she said, pressing her nose up against the pane of clean glass as she gazed with wonder at a huge, furry fox. Lauren peeped over her daughter's shoulder and was forced to agree.

'Yes, he's lovely and has a lovely price tag to match too,' she said, pulling Beccy firmly away. Riccardo watched the scenario with attentive eyes.

On the other side of the reception area there was a huge man-made lake. It was teeming with all types of ducks, from the commonest mallard and moorhen to a lamentation of perfectly white swans that swam with majestic ease through the blue water. A path circled the lake, and they set off in unison to follow its direction. They decided to picnic on one of the grassy slopes that gave them a full view of the lake. Beccy could hardly wait to see the delights inside, and she was not disappointed. Riccardo flung open the hamper lid with an impresario air, and Beccy giggled at his antics. He flung a red checked tablecloth with remarkable skill at Lauren's stony face, catching her unawares. She glared at him, but the dazzling smile he offered in return made her stomach somersault and she lowered her eyes in defence.

'Hurry up, dreamer,' he said to her, continuing to empty the trove of goodies a top grocer had supplied. The array was marvellous, and Lauren felt her taste-buds tingle despite herself.

'This is great,' said Beccy with difficulty as she forced yet another cheesy cracker into her mouth.

'And now a little drink,' announced Riccardo, passing a soft fizzy drink to Beccy and producing a chilled bottle of crisp white wine for the adults. Lauren was going to refuse, but it was too late, and he handed her a glass, clinking the side with his own.

'To the future,' he whispered gently to her, a steely look in his dark eyes, and Lauren faltered as she lifted the glass to her soft mouth. He lay back on the soft grass, his eyes dancing with mischief as he talked freely to Beccy, telling her all about Florence and his life there.

'My city is the most beautiful in the whole of Italy, and yet I long to escape to the hills. The countryside that surrounds Florence is simply perfect. I have a second home now, near the Monastery of St Francis,' he began, turning his eyes on Lauren. She felt herself grow hot under his scrutiny and wondered if he remembered.

'There was a little cottage, practically a hovel, but it held special memories for me so I had it rebuilt with huge extensions, so now it is a beautiful home.'

Lauren couldn't help but remember the happy times she had known there, and her heart ached for a love she had never known. It seemed strange that Riccardo should go to such lengths to preserve a memory, but there again she had been one of many. Maybe he still took women there, only now it was more exclusive than the simple place she had known.

After everyone had eaten enough, the scraps were gathered together to feed the hungry brood of birds that had gathered for their meal. Lauren fed the gathering swans with uninterest, pulling at the bread with her fingers and scattering the crumbs with a resolute air. Beccy preferred the ducks that dived and pushed each other for a tiny morsel. Occasionally Lauren would watch Riccardo and Beccy laughing together at the antics of the ducks. They both seemed so at ease with one another—just as father and daughter should be, yet it was something she had never known.

Lauren sighed. Was it fair to take Beccy's father away from her? Was she justified or merely embittered by her own experiences? The pains of the past still haunted her with nightmarish realism. Riccardo watched Lauren, her empty eyes staring vacantly ahead as the swans grew closer and closer.

'What's the matter?' he whispered gently to her as he stood behind her, and Lauren could feel the gathering swell of tears pushing against the backs of her eyes. How could she tell him, tell him about her life? It was a complete contrast to his. Where he had wealth, she had only known poverty, in contrast to his happy, carefree childhood she had suffered at the hands of a cruel, violent man. She couldn't tell him; she was too ashamed of what she had caused. He sensed her misery and drew her slender body against his. She could feel the length of his body against her spine, and with traitorous familiarity her weakened frame curled into his, fitting together like a well-known jigsaw. He wrapped his arms around her tiny waist, the warmth and strength of his hands causing her stomach to contract violently. She rested against him, enjoying the strength she derived from his body.

'Tell me?' he coaxed, his smoky voice washing over her. She could feel his soft lips touching her ear with teasing sexuality. He pulled her even closer towards him and she knew the windcheater had failed miserably as a fortress against him.

'Don't,' she pleaded, not wishing him to see the effect he had on her, yet he was too clever to be fooled.

'Don't what?' he mocked as he allowed his mouth to trail across her ear, sending a fire through her limbs.

'It's not fair, Riccardo, it's not right.'

'Fair? Right?' he questioned her softly. 'All's fair in love and war,' he reminded her, pressing his hard body against her ever-yielding frame.

'Which is this, Riccardo?' she said numbly, her eyes darting to her daughter. He felt her head move and followed her gaze.

'Love,' he answered emphatically. 'We both love Beccy, my daughter,' he said seriously. Lauren's heart sank, though she wasn't sure why; what did she expect or want—surely not his love?

'It will take time. Beccy needs time before we tell her,' she told him, unable to see the angry gleam in his eyes.

'Beccy or you?' he asked with cutting precision.

'Both of us, Riccardo, we both need time. We all need time,' she said wearily, thinking of the impossible situation she was in.

'You've had time, ten years of time,' he commented, the pain deep in the warm timbre of his voice.

Lauren turned to face him and found they were too close for comfort. An inner voice was warning her to draw back, yet she couldn't, and she despised herself for her weakness. His arms had wrapped around her with characteristic ease, and she was trapped in his steel grip. She knew she was blushing, she could feel the heat on her face, and she caught the laughter in his eyes as he looked down on her. He was still serious but his face held a tenderness she hadn't expected, and the effect it had on her frightened her.

'Let me go,' she pleaded as she tried to pull away from the hunger that was swirling in the depths of his ebony eyes. He raised his eyebrows with a cool air of superiority.

'I did that once before and you robbed me of my dearest possession,' he warned her quietly. Lauren lowered her head; she couldn't bear to see the accusation in his eyes. 'We will marry and be a family,' he added with satisfaction.

Lauren felt cold; an icy dread and haunting childhood memories tormented her, and she pulled away, fighting against his strength with everything she possessed.

'It wouldn't work; you can't just marry for the sake of a child,' she cried, unaware of the speculative look Beccy was giving them both.

'I shall have my child,' he stated grimly as he strode away, catching Beccy by the hand and breaking into a run.

For a few seconds Lauren was transfixed, then she gave a scream as she flew after them, shouting at them to stop. Riccardo turned, swinging Beccy high into the air till her laughter filled the quiet stillness of the sanctuary. Lauren drew up beside them as he placed Beccy safely back on to the ground.

'Don't ever do that again,' spat Lauren, panting hard as she viewed him with unconcealed contempt.

'Do what?' he teased, the anger in his own face matching hers. 'Remember just how long ten years is,' he warned her, the underlying threat in his voice searing her soul.

'I think we had better go.' The grim finality in Lauren's voice brooked no argument. Beccy began to protest, but Riccardo took her arm firmly.

'We shall do as your mother wishes, young lady,' he told her sharply, and though his voice was stern it held a trace of humour. Lauren expected the protests to continue—they usually did. However, she was disappointed. Beccy responded immediately, though her face was crestfallen and her bottom lip drooped.

'I hope you're not sulking,' laughed Riccardo, but Beccy flounced off, tossing her blonde hair behind her with a gesture so like her mother's that he laughed even louder.

'Go back to the car—I'll get the hamper,' he told Lauren, leaving her to chase after Beccy. It seemed an age before Riccardo returned, although his long strides across the car park meant he was soon at their side. Lauren nodded her head in the direction of Beccy, who was resting on the car, her head down and a frown on her little face.

'I suppose you haven't enjoyed yourself?' he asked her teasingly, and Lauren hated the familiar ease he seemed to have with her daughter despite only just meeting her. Beccy said nothing, but drew a pattern in the dirt with the toe of her shoe.

'That being the case,' continued Riccardo, not perturbed in the least, 'I don't suppose you want to keep this as a memento.' He drew a concealed package from his bag and, with a flourish that annoyed Lauren, produced from it the furry fox. Beccy rushed towards him, flinging her arms around his neck and swinging on him. He hugged her back with an intensity that was derived from the years he had not known her. He looked across at Lauren, but she turned away, too hurt and too angry to acknowledge the cosy image.

The drive back was quieter—Beccy seemed happy enough to sit gazing out of the window, her arm wrapped tightly around the fox.

'What are you going to call him?' he asked, glancing in his mirror to see his daughter's happy face.

'Riccardo,' she answered back promptly.

The smile that creased Riccardo's face vanished as Lauren said scathingly, 'How apt.' The coldness of her remark was wasted on Beccy, but Riccardo stiffened, his face taut with anger.

The rest of the journey was conducted in an angry silence, and Lauren was grateful when they finally drew up outside her house. Her hope that Riccardo would drop them off and leave was wasted; he wanted to come in, and she could tell by his austere expression that he was determined to. Beccy hurried off to show her gift to her friend a couple of doors down, leaving them alone. Lauren filled the kettle—not that she wanted him to stay for coffee, but it gave her something to do rather than face him. She could feel his eyes boring into her back, hard and serious.

'I want her to know that I am her father before we marry,' he said suddenly, his words bouncing round the tiny kitchen and through Lauren's head with such force that for a moment she was stunned. She clung to the rim of the sink, her mind filled with dread. If only he knew her—*really* knew her—he wouldn't want a family with her. Didn't he know that to marry would be fateful? She destroyed families, not made them. She swung round to meet the anger in his face; his cruel, resolute mouth was a firm, hard line.

'There has to be another solution,' she said shakily, her eyes wide with fear as he gave her a slow cruel smile.

'There is—a court case; you lose, I win and, if your daughter can ever forgive you for abandoning her, maybe, just maybe, at eighteen she will wish to find you,' he taunted, the bitterness so clearly defined in every line on his hard face.

Lauren was locked into immobility; she stared numbly at him, unable to move. She couldn't live without Beccy, she couldn't bear the thought of her daughter's rejection. Her shoulders sagged; he seemed to be holding every card—then, desperate to remain in control, she thought of marriage.

'Mitchell,' she cried; from deep within her came a glimmer of hope. 'Mitchell...he and I will marry—she'll have a father then,' she countered.

The darkness that fell across his face frightened her more than anything she had ever seen in her life. She heard him draw a rough breath then expel it with a low, droning sound that echoed around her, dragging her down with the weight of her own guilt.

'Never!' he roared like a powerful, angry lion; every muscle in his body seemed to grow with the harsh sound of his voice. Instinct told Lauren to flee, but fear trapped her desperately to the spot. His face went pale, almost a deathly white beneath his usually bronzed skin. The hatred he felt for her shot from his eyes, piercing her soul with its intensity, and she saw the pain that underlay his anger, yet she was not moved by it. He had had his chance all those years ago; perhaps even now a word of love might have softened her, but there was only a terrible hatred between them across a sea of pain.

She stared at him, calling his bluff, defying his anguished, 'Never!' but he turned and marched away. She sighed as she heard the door slam, its reverberations echoing around the empty house with a deathly finality. She sank wearily on to a breakfast stool, her head sinking miserably into her hands. Had he believed her? she wondered. How far would she have to go to convince him— surely not marriage to Mitchell?

She was too absorbed in the sheer horror of what had passed between them to hear the frantic knocking at her door, and she jumped as she heard Beccy call. Her voice sounded strange, upset, and Lauren panicked—had

Riccardo tried to abduct her? She rushed for the door, flinging it wide and pulling Beccy into her arms.

'Get off me,' spat Beccy as tears filled her eyes, and she struggled for her freedom. Lauren dropped her hands immediately and stared in disbelief at the hurt, angry look on her daughter's face.

'You lied,' she sobbed, 'you lied. I do have a father, and he does love me.'

Lauren's stomach curled into a ball; she could see the pain, and she knew she had caused it.

'How do you know?' she asked, blinking back the tears that were filling her eyes.

'Riccardo, my father, told me,' she retorted proudly, glaring at her mother with angry intent.

Lauren was stunned; she had underestimated his determination.

'Beccy, Beccy, darling, let me explain,' she pleaded as she tried to draw her little girl towards her; but it was a fruitless exercise. Beccy drew away, and the hatred in her eyes caused Lauren to cry out. Her hand flew to her face in horror.

'What can I do?' she wailed hopelessly. 'What can I do? You must understand.'

Beccy stared at her mother, her body rigid and defiant. 'Marry him,' was her simple ultimatum.

CHAPTER FIVE

THE crisp knock on the door made Lauren jump. She couldn't understand her nerves—after all, she had invited him. She checked around the room again; she wanted it to look cosy and homely, but not too much—Riccardo might get the idea she was trying to seduce him, and nothing could be further from her mind.

She opened the door and shivered despite the warm clothes she was wearing. It was like standing before a blast of icy winter wind looking into his glacial features, but the gleam of triumph in his cold eyes was still apparent.

'You'd better come in,' said Lauren ungraciously, stepping back to allow him to enter and flicking her wealth of blonde hair from her face.

He dwarfed the hallway, and his close proximity alerted Lauren to the physical strength of the man. She followed him, noting the clean cut of his expensive suit and the shine on his soft leather shoes. The aroma of his aftershave seemed to hang in the air, still as enticing as ever, she thought miserably as she entered the living-room. She had chosen some quiet music, hoping it would pacify the antagonism between them, but she admitted ruefully to herself that that hardly seemed likely. She had prepared a simple meal, and arranged for Beccy to stay the night at a friend's. It was essential they were alone. They had so much to discuss, and Lauren, though forced to marry, wanted to make sure he understood her terms.

He sat down, stretching his long, muscular legs out; he looked so relaxed as he closed his eyes and listened to the music. For a moment, with his features in repose, he looked so familiar—like the laughing Riccardo she had once known.

She sighed. It was all so long ago; both of them had changed so much that it was impossible for them to re-capture their lost love. Defeat and frustration coiled up inside her like a tight spring. He had won, and she now had no alternative but to marry him—to do otherwise would destroy her relationship with Beccy forever. How could she ever have loved a man like that? He was hard and cruel and seemed bent on revenge—why else would he want to marry her? Lauren knew with a sure certainty that she hated Riccardo now more than she had ever done.

'So you agree?' he asked her, a velvet teasing quality in his voice that irritated her. He was now alert, watching her intently, his dark eyes glittering with amusement at her obvious discomfort.

Lauren nodded numbly; her mouth was too dry to confirm her acceptance verbally. She looked at his face, hard and unrelenting, with no trace of the man she had known. He had been bright and cheerful, full of life and fun; this man was hard and bitter.

'I agree to marry you,' she said quietly, 'but...' She faltered as his eyes grew darker. 'I'll be your wife in name only,' she finished. He remained unmoved, and Lauren wondered whether he had understood the statement she had just made. 'You understand what I mean?' she added, her pale eyes darting to his, still seeking the warmth she had once known.

'I understand perfectly,' he mimicked, drawing closer to her and grabbing her wrist in a vice-like grip. The pain shot up her arm and she gave a cry as she tried to pull free. 'Make your mind up, Lauren. Either you become my wife in every sense of the word or I shall just take Beccy.'

There was no choice, and he knew it. Beccy had grown more attached to him since finding out the truth, and it was obvious to Lauren that she was often deliberately excluded from their fun as some sort of punishment. Beccy was too young to understand the pain she was causing, but it didn't make it any easier to bear. Lauren lowered her head in defeat.

'You win, Riccardo,' she whispered hoarsely in a weary voice. 'I'll marry you, be your wife.' She paused to swallow the bitter gall in her throat. 'In every way,' she concluded grimly, a look of distaste on her face.

She saw the flash of anger in his eyes at her words, his mouth twisted into a humourless smile.

'I can assure you it will not be the ordeal you imagine,' he mocked her, stroking his hand up her arm, leaving a trail of fire in its wake. 'See how your body springs to life at my touch,' he mused, taking delight in the traitorous way her body behaved. She tried to move away, but her body had grown weak at his touch, and she felt her defences melt as he drew her into his arms.

'Lauren,' he whispered huskily as her soft breasts fell against his chest. She bit into her bottom lip, still trying to remain immune to his masterly strokes. His hands stroked slowly over her body, carefully moulding her weakening frame to his until she could feel the hardness of his body against hers. Her body trembled with anticipation, her skin becoming alive with every touch. He crushed her so closely to him that she could feel the slow beat of his heart against her own in a mutual rhythm that sounded like beautifully composed music. Their lips sought each other and met in a lightness that she had not dreamed possible. There was no anger in his persuasive kiss—it was tormentingly gentle and slow.

Lauren felt herself moulding her body even closer to his; their union was all she sought. She clung to him desperately, her pulses leaping as she felt his hand wrap possessively around her breast. She shuddered as he squeezed her gently, his thumb brushing lightly on the rounded curve of her raised nipple. She was lost in a whirlpool of desire, drowning in the uncharted depths of her very being. She knew she was kissing him back with a fervour and hunger that he had so expertly unleashed in her. She felt wild and abandoned. She knew she should stop, that she was playing a dangerous game, but her body refused to acknowledge the sensible reasoning of her brain.

She was surprised when he stopped suddenly, drawing back from her, and she felt an icy coldness at the space between them. His breath was as erratic as hers, and for a moment they both silently acknowledged the surprising attraction they felt for each other.

Riccardo was first to recover.

'I told you you would find it easy to comply with my wishes,' he mocked, viewing her with a sensuous grin.

'There's no need to gloat,' she informed him coldly, embarrassed by her body's betrayal.

'I'm not gloating, just delighted that at least one aspect of our marriage will be a success,' he taunted.

'I wanted something . . .' Lauren began.

'Already playing the role of a demanding wife?' he ridiculed playfully, and Lauren knew she couldn't tell him, not now. 'Well, what do you want?' he asked, suddenly curious when he saw the shadow of sorrow on her pale face.

'Let's eat first, open the wine,' she called as she went into the kitchen. Her mind was racing; she had had every intention of remaining immune to him yet she knew she was unable, and hated herself for it. She wanted Beccy to think them happily married so she would not have the burden of guilt she herself carried. She had to tell him that she expected his complaisance, but his temper was formidable and she doubted that they could live together without arguing. There was too much rancour between them, and although, as he had so clearly demonstrated, their sex life would be good it was hardly a basis for marriage.

Lauren busied herself taking the prepared casserole from the oven. It was an excellent meal, thick chunks of chicken cooked slowly in an abundance of garlic and red wine and tarragon. She tossed a simple fresh salad and offered him some hot crusty bread. It seemed strange to sit together after all this time. She had placed two candles on the table but had removed them at the last minute in case he considered it a romantic notion. This marriage was hardly made in heaven, she mused as she placed the food on the table.

They ate in silence, Lauren stealing hidden looks at Riccardo. She had to admit he was as handsome as ever—perhaps even more so. He now looked more mature, and the little grey that touched his temples gave him a distinguished air. He was enjoying his meal, Lauren could tell, and she was pleased. When she had first met him she had known nothing about food, and Riccardo had taken delight in introducing her to the delights of Italian cooking.

She picked at her own food, her mind too preoccupied with other thoughts. She had to tell him the truth, but it was so hard, and she didn't know how he

would react. She didn't want his pity, but she was afraid
that he would consider his own child tainted by her family
background.

She kept taking great gulps of wine to quell her anxiety.
Riccardo watched at first with amusement, but it was
quickly replaced with concern, and as Lauren filled her
glass yet again he grew angry.

'Is this whole affair so painful that you have to be
drunk to suffer my company?' he growled suddenly,
making her jump, and a splash of red wine ran across
the white cloth like spilt blood.

How apt, thought Lauren, watching the wine spread;
it reminded her of a sacrifice. She stiffened at his sharp
tone; she wanted to tell him but the words died on her
lips—it was her secret. He sighed audibly, and put down
his cutlery in order to reach out and touch her hand.

'What is it?' he questioned; he couldn't bear her like
this—racked with hidden thoughts that frightened him.
'Lauren?' he asked again, taking her hand as he rose
and pulling her over to the couch. 'Sit down,' he said
wearily, dropping to her side. 'Now what is it?'

Lauren shook her head and bit into her bottom lip as
she tried to formulate the words. He waited, watching
her; this he could not take. He liked her with fire, and
she looked now like the girl he had first known—oddly
vulnerable and distant. The pain was etched deeply on
to her face and her eyes held a far-away look as if her
mind was deep in the past, a troubled past.

'I've lied to you,' she confessed in a low voice, not
daring to look at him. She didn't want to see his angry
face; it would prevent her from continuing, and she had
to tell him to rid herself of the weight of this burden.

He said nothing, his mind racing as he tried to think straight; surely she didn't mean Beccy? That was impossible.

'Lied?' he echoed. 'About what?' A chill stole across his heart as he took her small cold hand in his, sensing the depth of her unhappiness and feeling strangely drawn to her. He wanted to comfort her, to ease the heartache she was suffering.

'My family, my mother, my father, even my brother—they aren't coming to the wedding,' she said numbly. It seemed strange to admit it to him—he had so readily believed her all those years ago. 'They don't, they don't...' The sobs that racked her body caused him a pain so deep that it seared through him, sharp and deliberate. Her pain was his, and he felt her sorrow with equal depth. He pulled her into his arms, trapping her shuddering body as the hot tears flooded down her cheeks.

'They don't approve of your decision to marry?' he coaxed as he rocked her, unable to comprehend such disappointment, such an excess of emotion—it was hardly a marriage she was entering willingly.

'They don't exist,' she wept. 'They don't damn well exist,' she sobbed again, leaving Riccardo lost. Her head fell heavily against his chest and her hot, salty tears made his wet shirt cling even tighter to his strong chest.

'There, now,' he consoled her, allowing her to cry her obvious grief away. 'Was there an accident?' he asked quietly after a time, thinking that some awful tragedy had wiped out her family, and finally understanding the depth of her grief.

Her head shot up; her pale blue eyes were surrounded by red rings of anguish. Her face was troubled and there

was an anger in her so deep that he knew there was something seriously wrong.

'What is it?' he asked, but she was too distraught to
hear the concern in his voice. 'Was there an accident?'
he persisted, not understanding the tortuous expression
on her face.

'Yes,' she said vehemently, 'me.' Then she fell back
again and cried and cried till she could cry no more.

It was several hours later before the whole dismal story
was told, and Riccardo's reaction changed from anger
at her parents to dismay at the lack of help available to
Lauren as she had struggled to adjust to her life in care.
He was gentle and as understanding as he could be, but
the revelation had shocked him, and he now had an in-
sight about her.

'My poor, poor Lauren,' he whispered softly, stroking
her damp curls from her face. 'Why did you never tell
me?' he asked as he held her against him, holding her
tightly to block out any further pain.

'I'm a failure; it was all my fault. My parents' marriage broke up because of me, my foster placements
broke down because of me. I was just so ashamed,' she
sobbed, clinging to him for support, as the dam burst
on all her pent-up feelings.

Riccardo sighed loudly.

'It was not your fault,' he said firmly. 'You have been
so unlucky, but none of those things was your fault,' he
reassured her, wondering if she believed him. 'Lauren,
there's no need to worry; I love Beccy. Don't ever
think . . .' he began.

'No, no, it's all right; I know you'll never hurt Beccy—
not like that, but . . .' she faltered; she knew Riccardo
would never take out his frustrations on his daughter.

He was not that type of man. But then she was seized by another worry.

'We don't love each other; as she gets older she will know that the only reason we married was for her.' She began to cry again, thinking of the pain she had suffered, the pain and guilt of forcing together parents who would rather be apart.

'We can tell her we do love each other,' he said simply. 'Oh, Lauren,' he sighed, still holding her close and stroking her long blonde hair.

She relaxed against the comforting warmth of his chest and closed her eyes; suddenly she felt so very tired. She inhaled purposely so she could enjoy the familiar, reassuring scent of the man. The solid rhythm of his heartbeat and the gentle movement of his chest as it rose and fell with every breath lulled her into a gentle sleep. Riccardo allowed her to stay there, stroking her hair as he thought about what he had been told.

'Come on, sleepy head, let's put you to bed,' he said, sitting up. The hours that had passed had made him stiff, and he knew she would sleep better in bed. He carried her upstairs with surprising ease. She was too weak to protest, tired out by the exertion of releasing all her pent-up emotions. He undressed her with care and she was too numb to care; her body flopped against him like a rag doll. He pulled her nightdress over her head, watching the delicate material fall over her slender body with appreciation. He began to cover her up, but she started protesting again.

'But it would be a lie, another lie, to pretend we love each other—you understand, don't you?' she said wearily as her eyelids began to droop, the effects of the wine beginning to take their toll. 'We would be living a lie.'

'Would it be a lie?' he asked, but she was already asleep. He bent down and kissed her lightly on her forehead and wiped away a tear that still clung to her cheek, glistening like a newly cut diamond. He stared at her for several moments; he wanted to erase her past, to wash away all the unnecessary guilt she was carrying. Yet he knew that, in the final analysis, it was Lauren herself who had to come to terms with her past.

Some memories of that night were still unclear to Lauren several days later, although she perceived a change in Riccardo and she wondered what exactly had passed between them. He had obviously put her to bed, but was there more? she thought. Nevertheless there was a freedom in truth that she had not expected—she felt relieved that he knew about her past. The huge burden she had carried for so long, her hidden secret that she was so ashamed of, had now finally been aired.

Beccy was in a high state of excitement as the wedding-day drew nearer. She had been delighted that she was chosen to be bridesmaid, and loved the beautiful pink taffeta dress that she was to wear. At first Lauren had protested against a flamboyant wedding, wanting a simple affair—they were hardly young lovers after all. But Riccardo had been furious.

'My family are travelling from Italy—they will expect a church wedding,' he told her.

'But it's so silly. We have a ten-year-old daughter—I can hardly wear white,' she countered.

'Then wear ivory or cream, but I want you to look every inch a bride. We shall marry with pride—lovers reunited with the added bonus of a child,' he warned her.

'But...'

'No buts; if we marry any other way people will suspect our motives, and we would not want that to happen. Think of Beccy,' he reminded her.

She was defeated again, yet she was thrilled with her dress, and the wedding would have been perfect, she was forced to admit, had they loved each other.

On the day itself she began the long walk up the aisle, Beccy receiving as many compliments as her. She saw Riccardo turn to look at her, and for a moment she caught a glimpse of the man she had known. He smiled at her, his white teeth flashing and his eyes dancing with delight. She returned the smile, realising he was merely playing a part, as she must do too.

The wedding reception was arranged to be held in a top London hotel, the bridal suite had been booked for the night, and rooms for every guest who required overnight accommodation. Lauren and Riccardo were greeted with chilled champagne and a flurry of congratulations. Riccardo, playing the part of happy bridegroom with remarkable ease, wrapped his arm around Lauren's waist, drawing her closer to him.

'Smile brightly, darling,' he hissed through clenched teeth as Lauren gazed miserably at the crowd of people Riccardo called family, his grip on her waist tightening as he spoke. She responded immediately, smiling and nodding her thanks to a seemingly endless line of people.

Once the formalities were over, the wedding breakfast was far less formal. Riccardo had arranged an elaborate buffet and the flow of champagne was ceaseless. Lauren passed between the family groups, amazed by their overt warmth. Yet she knew no one, and Riccardo was too busy introducing Beccy to all her newly found relatives. She felt alone, strangely out of place at her own wedding.

'Penny for them?' a familiar friendly voice broke into her thoughts, and she smiled immediately.

'I didn't think you would come,' she admitted, the relief evident in her voice.

'Of course—I wanted to see what he had that I didn't,' laughed Mitchell. 'Now I know what: good looks and extreme wealth. I can't compete.' He smiled ruefully, but she could hear the sorrow in his voice.

'He's Beccy's father,' Lauren stated, trying to ignore the stunned look on Mitchell's face. 'It was either marry him or lose Beccy, and I couldn't do that,' she confessed glumly, unaware that Riccardo was approaching.

'Do you think that was a good idea, Lauren?' Mitchell asked suddenly, concerned, a puzzled look on his face. Lauren shook her head dumbly; she wasn't sure of anything any more.

'You don't mind if I take my wife?' growled Riccardo, coming between them and grasping Lauren's arm. Mitchell stared, and Lauren pleaded silently to him to say nothing.

'You can forget that!' Riccardo spat out, drawing her over to a quiet corner seat away from the hullabaloo. 'You're my wife now, and I won't be humiliated by you a second time,' he warned her, his dark eyes narrowing dangerously.

Lauren took the full impact of his words in a shocked silence. Did he think so little of her that she would have an affair—worse than that, embark upon one at her wedding reception? Her anger flared, bringing an un-characteristic glow to her face.

'How dare you?' she cried indignantly, keeping her voice low so as not to alert the guests.

'Your outrage does you proud—you'd even convince me if I didn't know you better,' he scoffed. 'However, it is of little consequence as we shall be in Italy to-morrow,' he informed her, enjoying the stunned look on her face.

'Italy?' she repeated, trying to keep the surprise from her voice. 'We're going to take a honeymoon?' She sneered at the ridiculousness of it.

He shook his head, his dark hair falling momentarily in his face before he tossed it back with an air of disdain.

'Not a honeymoon—we are going to live there,' he said slowly, as if explaining to a child. Lauren frowned as his words sank in; surely he couldn't be serious? But the look on his face seemed to lack humour.

'I'm not going to live in Italy,' she said hurriedly, determined to be firm on this point.

He shrugged his powerful shoulders in uninterest, as if it were of no consequence, and Lauren relaxed and allowed herself a smile.

'You agree, then, we stay in England?' She wanted his confirmation; he was too calm, too confident.

'If you wish to give our daughter the impression of a happy marriage, I should have thought remaining with your husband was one of the most important points,' he mocked.

Lauren's eyes narrowed. How heartless could he be? She couldn't go just like that, uproot herself and Beccy. She gave a cry.

'What about Beccy? This is her home,' she tried to plead with him, to make him understand; but his face remained emotionless and he viewed her with glacial eyes.

'Beccy is looking forward to the prospect of living in Italy,' he informed her, suddenly clasping her by the waist and drawing them closer together.

'What the . . . ?' protested Lauren.

'Appearances—we must look like a newly wed couple,' he said, holding her tightly.

Lauren tried to move, but the light in his eyes warned her to be still. It was hard sitting so close to him, especially today, as he had never looked more handsome. The dark grey morning suit fitted him to perfection. It gave him an aristocratic air which suited his arrogance, thought Lauren.

'You were saying?' he asked, fixing his dark eyes on her and staring intently at her face; to anyone looking on he would have appeared the besotted husband.

'Beccy has to go to school.'

'Of course, but surprise, surprise, we have schools in Italy.' He was goading her, enjoying her discomfort.

'There's my job,' she returned immediately, already knowing she was beaten.

He nodded as if considering it, then said thoughtfully, 'It is of no importance.'

Lauren was furious; she had worked hard to achieve that position, and he dismissed it out of hand. She pulled away from him, struggling to stand in the acres of old silk that billowed around her slim legs.

'I will not give up my job! I had to give up all my youth while my friends were enjoying college, going out at night, having fun. I was stuck at home with a child, struggling with night classes and part-time work so I could get a good job. I've worked damned hard for that job—more than you could ever realise. I will not just give it up and become a full-time wife to massage your ego,' she stated with as much conviction as she could muster under his penetrating gaze.

He gave her a cruel smile and shrugged expressively.

'My daughter and I leave in two days. The choice is yours,' he added—as if allowing her an option, she

thought angrily as she walked away. She managed to
avoid Riccardo for quite a time after that, but he soon
found her again.

'It is inappropriate that we be separated for any length
of time,' he said hoarsely to her, moving a stray tendril
of hair that had fallen from her elaborate style on to her
face. This simple gesture she found strangely touching,
and she cast a covert glance at him. He was looking down
at her, his expression surprisingly at odds with the
sharpness in his voice.

'Have you eaten yet?' he asked; he knew she hadn't—
she had wandered around aimlessly, taking little interest
in the wedding breakfast. Lauren shook her head and
her hair fell again. He pushed it back behind her ear,
his touch warm, and he let his hand caress her neck for
a moment. Lauren shivered at his touch, and he acknowledged it with a knowing smile that coloured her
cheeks.

'Come on, I'll get you something.' He pulled her gently
across the floor to the long tables that took up one half
of the hall. It was an impressive display—ice carvings
of Cupid stood three feet high. Lauren looked with
interest at them, amused by their cheeky grins and marvellous detail.

'It's a pity they melt,' she said, half to herself, then
she added wistfully, 'Doesn't all love fade in the end?'

'Really, Lauren, you are depressing for a bride,' he
criticised her, the laughter in his voice unmistakable.

'We're hardly the ideal couple—lovers we are not,'
she said emphatically, helping herself to a plate and
looking around for something tasty to eat.

'But we will be,' he promised her, and the soft silkiness
of his voice unnerved her. Lauren moved further away,

but he was by her side in seconds, plying her plate with an array of little bites.

'Don't worry, I have ordered a late supper to be delivered to our suite just in case you need fortifying,' he told her.

Lauren swung round to face him. 'I shan't need fortifying because nothing is going to happen,' she snapped.

His dark eyes glittered with cruel satisfaction.

'Well, let's see, shall we?' he tormented her as he drew closer, taking the plate from her hand and putting it down on to the table. He took her roughly into his arms, and the initial struggle she attempted was soon quelled by the firmness of his grip.

She would not give him the satisfaction of fighting him, she thought; she would remain aloof, stiff, unresponsive, she decided as she watched his face draw closer till it was completely blurred. She kept her mouth firmly shut, refusing to respond to his hard lips. He grew more aggressive; his mouth became harder and he forced her lips apart with a brutality she had not thought possible, and continued to kiss her, making her aware of his strength and power.

He fused their bodies together, and the effect was electric—she could feel how much he wanted her, and the thought made her weaken. One minute the kiss was a cruel paradox, the next a passionate embrace; she kissed him back, probing his mouth with her tongue, teasing his lips with a gentleness that made him moan, and his grip tightened still further. They were in their own world, oblivious to the watching audience.

It was the laughter and applause that drew them back, and they stared at each other with unconcealed hunger in their eyes. Riccardo laughed and wrapped his arms around her.

'She's beautiful, isn't she?' he asked the amused guests, and Lauren felt strangely elated by his words— even if he didn't mean them, she thought. She blushed as the guests viewed them, obviously delighted by this show of affection. She was terrified; she had given him so much already—first Beccy, then her job and the life she had known. She had given him everything—or had he taken it? She wasn't sure, but on one point she was determined. She would not allow him to make love to her; she must retain some dignity, she thought as she looked again at the clock, dreading the moment that was drawing ever closer.

'Are you so eager to be in bed?' the smoky voice of Riccardo laughed in her ear. 'Or do you watch the clock to see how much longer till your terrible fate arrives?'

'I don't see why we have to; I wouldn't mind you having a mistress—as long as you were discreet,' she added, suddenly feeling a momentary stab when she thought of him with someone else.

Riccardo shook her head and laughed with good humour.

'How generous you are, but, my little wife, you need have no fear. We shall both be faithful,' he said. The edge in his voice warned her that he was serious, and she shivered. Guests began to leave, wishing the happy couple good luck and the men winking and nudging each other like adolescent schoolboys. Lauren had already settled Beccy in her room, and she had fallen asleep the moment her head had touched the pillow. The band was still playing, but Lauren's feet ached, since she had been partnered for much of the evening. She yawned and covered her mouth, but she was too late.

'I think we should go to bed,' said Riccardo, enjoying the flush of colour that immediately covered her cheeks.

They stood to leave, and the band played a romantic ballad as they left the hall. Lauren walked up the stairs, pulling at her dress as she struggled along.

The bridal suite was even more beautiful than she had expected, and she gasped with surprise when she saw the huge bouquet of red roses that dominated the room. She turned and faced him.

'Thank you,' she said, pleased by his kind gesture, and the smile he gave her warmed her heart. She dropped her gaze immediately.

'I'll go down to the bar and have a drink—it will give you time to get ready,' he said, sensing her sudden embarrassment. She nodded and watched him leave.

It was difficult removing the wedding dress with nervous fingers. Lauren was determined to be asleep when he got back, as she knew he would not wake her. She showered in record time, removing her make-up and brushing her hair with a speed that surprised even herself. She went over to the bed; it was the epitome of romance—a huge bed, adorned with a lace canopy, and there lying in the centre was a large black box tied with a white ribbon. She knew immediately what it was; her fingers untied it and she pulled out a long silk négligé trimmed with creamy lace, and low-cut—the lace would barely cover her breasts.

It was beautiful, though, she had to admit as she stroked the fine fabric. She knew she would have to wear it, but as she would be asleep when he came up and certainly out of the bed before he awoke she felt safe. It fitted perfectly, moulding around her attractive figure with ease. The soft fabric made her feel strangely sensual, and she smoothed her hands over the material, enjoying the feel of it.

She climbed into bed and closed her eyes, turned on to her right side then her left. She tossed and turned but her mind was still racing and sleep was elusive. She heard the door open and stiffened, swallowing the lump of fear that was rising in her chest. She pulled the covers up to her ears and closed her eyes. She would pretend she was asleep.

She lay as still as she could and kept her eyes firmly closed. Her ears were straining, listening to every move he made. He seemed to undress with lightning speed and Lauren stiffened as the covers were drawn back and he slid into bed beside her. She could feel the heat from his body and knew instinctively, without looking, that he was naked.

'I know you're awake, Lauren,' he said mockingly as he moved beside her. He propped himself up on his elbow and leaned over her. She could feel the warmth of his breath on her face. She knew it was silly to pretend; she wasn't a child any more, she was not the girl he knew, she was a fully mature adult even if he did so very often make her feel like a child. She turned in the bed angrily and met the amused grin on his face with a look of thunder.

'You can take that smug look off your face,' she informed him coldly, trying to forget the fact that his naked body seemed to draw a heat from her that made her long to look at him; but she kept her eyes firmly on his face. 'I've told you before, this pretence of marriage stops at the bedroom door.' She tried to make her voice firm and aggressive, but it was difficult. Riccardo's eyes had begun to trail over her body with a hunger that excited her, and she suffocated her own desires, which were beginning to grow deep within her. He seemed oblivious to her objections as he ran his finger lightly over the lace trim, his fingers descending slowly towards her breasts, which already quivered with excitement. Lauren stiffened at his electric touch, her eyes wide with fear; she knew she would weaken, and had to stop him. She hit out, slapping his hand away from her body.

'Stop that,' she snapped angrily, turning away from him and pulling the covers over herself again. He laughed softly at her reaction as if he had been expecting it.

He planted a gentle kiss on her shoulder, and she tried to ignore the warmth his kiss gave her as he whispered, 'Lauren, we made a deal, remember? You are to be my wife in every sense of the word,' he added, a smoky, suggestive teasing in his words that made Lauren swallow nervously.

He wrapped his arm around her waist and felt her stomach contract. 'Don't stiffen up on me, Lauren.' The censure in his voice sent a *frisson* of fear down her spine, but she remained unmoved, determined not to give in despite the flurry of emotions that he was arousing within her. She tried to wrench herself away, but he was too quick and his arm tightened fiercely around her waist, drawing her backwards till her body was curled up against his. She tried to control the panic that was rising within her, threatening to engulf her sanity.

'Riccardo,' she protested, her voice lacking the conviction it had had before; but he held her in a vice-like grip. She could feel his body hardening with desire as he moved sensuously against her own. A hot flush of colour seeped over Lauren's face; she knew he was deliberately teasing her. His voice was warm and persuasive as he crooned her name in her ear. Yet she could sense the anger that lay beneath the surface and she was amazed at her own responses to him. The blood was rushing through her body till her flesh seemed to burn.

'Stop it,' she demanded, but he took no heed, and Lauren could feel her own defences weakening. There was a low rumble of laughter from him at her rebellion. She tried to remain unresponsive as his hands stroked over her body, but his masterful hands were awakening in her desires she had kept hidden for so long. She began to wriggle, to move her body away, to fight his superior strength.

'Keep still, Lauren,' he threatened, 'or do you prefer it that way?' he taunted as she arched her back and struggled for her freedom. She began to kick wildly, her body writhing. He saw the brief flash of anger in her eyes and smiled at her. She stilled in his arms. His breath was hot on her face and she could see the blazing hunger in his eyes as he looked down on her. Desperately she struggled once more against his body. The flame of passion was flaring in his dark depths as he held her down on the bed.

'I want you, Lauren,' he told her softly as he pinned her down, the weight of his body pressing down on her. She began to wriggle again; balling her hands into hard fists, she beat on his back till her arms ached.

'Go on,' he mocked savagely, 'fight me all you want. It's better than you lying there like a rag doll,' he growled, the contempt for her apparent as he pulled at her silky négligé. She heard the material tear and experienced the coldness of being laid naked before a man who felt nothing for her except the need to satisfy his own desire.

Was this his revenge for taking his daughter from him? Had they both gone so far that there was nothing between them? She could remember him still as the gentle lover she had known, skilfully enticing her innocent body to respond to him. She, once a tender, shy girl, was now as angry and as bitter as he. All they seemed to want to do was hurt each other.

'I'll not take you, Lauren,' he said smokily as his eyes burned into her body. 'I'll not take you till you beg,' he added with an assurance that made her body immediately stiffen, and she flushed with agitation.

He lowered himself gently upon her, kissing her lips with a tenderness she had not expected. He bent his head, moving slowly down to her swelling breasts, her nipples already erect with anticipation. Her body jerked with abandon as his tongue traced a ring of fire around her breasts. She had only ever made love once, and the reaction of her body still alarmed her. He wrapped his hand possessively around her breast, his thumb flicking against her nipple, rubbing its rosy peak till she moaned with pleasure.

Her body was alive, every nerve crying out for fulfilment. She had denied herself for so long that her body craved satisfaction. The desire to be satisfied was overwhelming, and she felt her body move rhythmically against his, pushing herself against his hardness. She could feel herself sinking into the depths of desire and she called out to him in a desperate attempt to prevent them going any further.

'Stop, Riccardo. There's enough hate between us,' she pleaded. He laughed cruelly, enjoying the heat and desire that was apparent in her eyes.

'Hate or love,' he mocked, 'there's little difference.'

His hands began a slow descent, stroking over her naked body towards her flat stomach. Her body buckled as his hands swept over her hips, drawing her upwards to his body.

'If you hate me so much, Lauren, why does your body quiver at my touch?' He laughed and she closed her eyes against his face, frightened of what he might see. She knew her body was traitorous, determined to be satisfied even though her brain screamed out its denial. She bit softly into her lips to trap the cry that bubbled up inside her as his hand slipped between her thighs. He was touching her with an intimacy that sent a blaze of desire through her.

'Don't do that,' she managed to say, but Riccardo paid no heed. 'No!' Her voice was high with panic as she felt him push her legs further apart. She was trapped and totally vulnerable. He lay at her side, supremely confident in his own superiority. She was unable to move; his legs pinned hers and his mouth descended on her lips to prevent any further protests. Dimly she was aware of him moving, his body suddenly on hers, the weight of him pressing down hard, and his hot lips seeking hers with a mutual hunger. An explosion of desire ripped through her as his tongue probed deeply, teasing her with his expert kisses. His hands had moved down the length of her body with long, unhurried strokes, curling around her hips, spanning the gentle curve of her bottom and pulling her gently upwards. When his mouth left her lips, his voice was husky and deep.

'Do you want me, Lauren?' he asked, his voice raw with emotion. He kissed her again, a long, demanding kiss forcing her lips to open, and a fierce blaze of desire made her shudder. She wrapped her arms around him, clasping his back and pulling him down on her. She moved her hips, seeking him, and moaned a soft complaint when he moved away. She pressed her nails deep into his back as his strong fingers teased her intimately, making her cry out with pleasure. She knew what he wanted, and still part of her tried to deny the impact of her feelings till she could take it no more.

'Riccardo,' she groaned.

'Yes?' he mocked, his voice deep and warm.

'Please, Riccardo,' she pleaded, moving against him with an abandon she had not thought possible.

'Riccardo!' The cry was torn from her; it was the final admission of defeat and surrender. All she could feel was the sheer pleasure and ecstasy of knowing her first love, her only love again, and for those moments she allowed herself to be transported back to that summer long ago when she had first known his love. She drowned in the memories, as their bodies fused together in a feverish frenzy of passion. She felt a brief sudden pain and for a moment stiffened, but it passed so quickly and her arousal was complete. It seemed an eternity before they were both fully satisfied. Afterwards she curled up against him, hiding in the crook of his arm, and fell into a deep, welcoming sleep.

CHAPTER SIX

THE moment she woke up, her heart sank. She still lay curled up beside him, and suddenly the night's events hit her. She darted a quick look at Riccardo—his face seemed strangely at peace and gentle—then quickly dropped her gaze as she realised he was already awake and was looking at her with such intensity that her stomach was a whirl of butterflies. She felt sick as last night's events came to mind with embarrassing clarity, and shut her eyes, trying to block out the memory.

'Good morning,' he said, the triumphant laughter in his voice making her blush.

'Good morning,' she managed to reply as she edged her body away from his, finding the closeness of his body disturbing. He moved quickly, drawing her back towards him and holding her next to him so close that she could hear the thudding beat of his heart filling her ears.

'Don't move; I want to talk, to thank you.' He spoke quietly, with a tenderness that made her heart soar, yet she couldn't help but be immediately defensive.

'Talk what about?' Her tone was sharp, and she heard him sigh when he heard it.

'Rebecca...' He was not allowed to say any more. Lauren sat up, her eyes blazing. She grasped the thin sheet to cover her body and her action was met with a smile of derision.

'What about Beccy?' she asked, suddenly panicking again. 'What have you done with her?' she asked frantically, already hating herself for the night before. She saw now that it was all a trick, a cruel hoax while he robbed her of her daughter.

Riccardo pulled her back towards him, wrapping a comforting arm around her.

'Nothing—I presume she is still in bed, but you always have to think the worst,' he said, a trace of sorrow in his voice. 'I just want to thank you for having my daughter—she is a credit to you.'

He sounded sincere, and Lauren felt a strange pride at his words. She relaxed, still a little unsure—the experience of last time had left too many questions in her mind.

'How were you when you were pregnant?' he asked, longing to know, to understand. He wanted to share those moments with her.

'I was fat and sick like everyone else,' she retorted bitterly, not trusting his sudden interest. She didn't like this; he made her feel vulnerable by his concern. She wanted to hate him, to carry on hurting him for all the pain he had made her suffer, yet already she knew she was weakening.

'Very sick?'

'No,' she said, shaking her head. 'Only at first, but after that I just ate and ate. I was enormous!' She laughed at the memory as the image of her waddling along like a duck sprang to mind.

'I can't imagine you fat,' he said huskily, allowing his hand to trace across her flat stomach. 'You're so slim now, as if you have never had a child,' he murmured as he looked at her body with interest. 'I still think I should have liked to see that,' he then said quietly, almost to himself.

'Seen what?' Lauren asked, puzzled, already aware that her body was awakening to his touch. Alarm bells immediately began ringing in her head.

'You pregnant, carrying my child,' he replied softly as he stroked her waist with a firm touch. 'I think to see a woman carrying a child is a beautiful sight, and you with my child must have been adorable.'

Lauren felt a glow for a moment, then remembered how he had first reacted to the news and dismissed it as a fanciful notion. She would have liked him there, though, loving her, awaiting the birth of their child. She swallowed the rising bitterness in her throat as she thought about how it had really been: her, totally alone and frightened.

She gave a shiver as the grey walls of the hospital flashed before her. She closed her eyes to shut out the memory and instinctively drew closer to his strength, as if her body was aware of the dark thoughts that were threatening to drown her.

'It couldn't have been easy for you, having no family,' he continued, perceptive enough to understand her re-action. He was fully aware that she might clam up immediately, and felt her recoil at the mention of family, so increased the soothing strokes on her body. He waited till he sensed her relax.

'You're a good mother to Rebecca—you should be proud of yourself,' he remarked, but there was a note of pride in his voice too that surprised her.

'Proud of myself?' she mocked questioningly. 'Why?'

He held her tighter and spoke with a firm but gentle voice.

'We learn most of our parenting skills by example. You never had that opportunity.' He paused to allow her to think about that, then added, 'That's why you should be proud. Proud that you never let your own experiences influence Rebecca. I presume you haven't told her the truth about your life because you want her to be free of such pain. I admire you greatly for that. It is so easy to want to share our pain to make it easier on ourselves.'

Lauren was silent; her mind was racing. She had always felt inadequate, a reject, but she had actually succeeded in something against all odds. She allowed herself a smile as she thought how different Beccy's childhood had been from her own, but would that happiness continue now she had married Riccardo?

He seemed to read her mind.

'I can't see why not—we both love her,' he interrupted her thoughts with amazing accuracy.

Lauren nodded in silent agreement and darted him a covert glance. He spoke of love so freely with Beccy, but never mentioned her. She tried to read the look in his eyes, but they were deep and unfathomable.

'We'd better go down for breakfast,' she said; suddenly she found this conversation disturbing.

He smiled in answer. 'Brides and grooms are served breakfast in bed.'

Lauren felt trapped; she wanted to hate him, she *had* to hate him—to acknowledge any other feeling would be disastrous. How long did she honestly expect this fiasco to go on? The marriage was doomed. She had seen it all before—the common bond of a child was never enough, and she knew sooner or later he would want them both out of his life. Being a father was a new experience for him, a novelty, but no doubt the novelty would wear off, especially if Beccy had one of her difficult days.

'I think I'll shower,' she said, sliding from his arms and pulling the sheet across her naked body. He grinned with amusement.

'It's a bit late for modesty.' He laughed then added lightly, grinning with amusement, 'And there's no door on the bathroom.'

Lauren coloured at the memory that had so conveniently slipped her mind. She dropped the sheet, refusing to be mocked by him, and he gave a deep, low gasp of appreciation as the sheet fell seductively around her slim ankles. She stood completely motionless; the stillness of her body was dramatically beautiful and she was enjoying the power she knew she had over him.

An unspoken message of desire seemed to transmit itself across the bed, each of them suddenly totally aware of the other with a yearning so deep that it was almost tangible. Riccardo leant across the bed to capture her, but she had moved with the same sudden grace to be with him. Their arms entwined as they locked their lips together in a hot embrace.

The passion of last night was replaced with a tantalising slowness. His caresses were leisurely and deliberate, and Lauren responded by touching him. At first her actions were tentative and cautious—she moved her fingers through the dark mat of hair that covered his muscular chest and smoothed her hands over the high ridge of his shoulders, moving them slowly down his spine, feeling his back, his muscles with deep sensitivity because she wanted to know every inch of the man.

He shuddered against her, moaning deep within his throat as her hands moved over the firm rise of his hips. She paused momentarily, still wary, before allowing her hands to trace downwards. He gave a moan of deep pleasure and moved closer. He was kissing her with in-

creased intensity as her hands explored his body. A heat
was warming them both as they sought ways of giving
each other pleasure, and their kisses were wonderfully
deep yet tender.

'Lauren,' he whispered huskily, his voice filled with
hungry desire as she stroked him till his body was stiff
against the supple gentleness of her own. His mouth
rained kisses on her eager face, smothering her lips with
a passion he could barely control. His caresses scorched
her, making the fire of desire spring to life, fanning her
passion. She clung to him, kissing him back with equal
fervour. Her tongue began to trace over his body; she
enjoyed the salty taste of his skin on her lips, and she
was intoxicated with the ability she had to arouse him.
They moved against each other, but she was determined
to remain in control this time. She wanted him to cry
out for her, to want her even if it was only to satisfy his
sexual appetite.

She drew a little away from him and began to tease
him, gently touching him with an intimacy she had never
thought possible. He groaned as he lay back, his arms
stretching out for her, pulling her back to him till her
swelling breasts fell heavily on top of him. She looked
down on his face; the bitterness and harshness had been
washed away by passion, and his eyes were closed, a smile
of pleasure curling his sensual mouth. She moved her
body over his, the softness of her breasts rubbing against
the rough dark hairs on his chest, her breasts aching
with desire as she moved rhythmically against him, increasing the erotic pleasure of the movement by allowing his hands to cup her breasts till he moaned with
pleasure and gripped her tightly. He found the erect peak
of her breast and teased her with his hot kisses.

She must be betraying herself—he must sense her love. *Did* she love him? the thought raced through her mind. To do so would be a fateful mistake; he had never loved her—even now their relationship was only for her daughter's sake.

He forced her off him, and gave a smile of triumph as she lay beneath his strong body. Then he began to kiss her again, a deep, warm kiss full of the hidden depths that ran beneath the surface. Their bodies were locked together—a closeness that nearly made them one.

They were unaware of the sharp knock on the door, and it was immediately flung open before they had a chance to respond. They both turned to see Beccy, an amused and knowing grin on her face as she looked at them both with curiosity born of interest. Riccardo rolled back away from Lauren and folded his arms across the back of his head as he viewed his daughter with a cool air of disapproval. Lauren felt a flush of colour to her cheeks.

'Beccy——' she began, but was immediately interrupted by Riccardo.

'It's polite to wait for an invitation before you come in,' he growled, his eyes narrowing as he viewed the unrepentant Beccy.

'I come in my mother's room every morning,' she flung back at him crisply before turning to her mother for support.

'You *used* to come,' Riccardo immediately corrected her, his voice low and firm.

Beccy glared at him, but he was unmoved by the angry look on her face. She turned to Lauren, who had sat in silence; she had been embarrassed herself by the interruption, and she was glad that Riccardo had pointed that out to Beccy. Still, it galled her to think he was taking over her daughter.

'Mum,' cried Beccy, the plea in her voice high and dramatic, and she made a move to come to the bed.

Lauren smiled as she approached but Riccardo immediately roared, 'Out—your mother and I shall be down presently.'

Hot tears immediately sprang to Beccy's eyes; Lauren could see the sorrow shining in them as the girl turned and fled. She made a dart to stop her, but Riccardo gripped her arm tightly to prevent her. She tried to pull free as she called out Beccy's name, but the door slammed and Lauren turned to face Riccardo.

'How dare you? Don't you ever speak like that to my daughter again,' she shouted, her eyes blazing as she viewed him with obvious disapproval.

'Our daughter,' he corrected her coolly as he flung back the covers in a gesture of contempt and left the bed.

'I won't have it, Riccardo. You have to understand that I will not have you disciplining my daughter. You've really upset her, you know,' she continued as she heard the sound of the shower filling the room.

Lauren frowned; he seemed immune to her point of view. This is the beginning, she thought grimly; already the novelty of being a father is wearing off.

She waited till he had finished showering, determined to confront him. He came from the bathroom completely relaxed; he was drying his hair with a towel and around his waist he had wrapped another one. Lauren felt herself colour as she recalled how close they had been, sharing an intimacy she had never imagined possible. He looked at her, sensing the angry tension within her, and sighed.

'OK, Lauren,' he said almost wearily, 'let's hear it.'

'I would prefer it, Riccardo, if you would leave the upbringing of Beccy to me.' She hoped that sounded reasonable—after all, she was her mother, the only parent she had known since her birth. The amusement that made his mouth quirk and show a flash of teeth did not, however, take the glacial look from his eyes. He looked at her, the black glitter of building anger apparent in his cool scrutiny.

'Lauren, Rebecca is my daughter—remember that,' he warned her softly, but she paid no heed to his request.

'I've spent the last ten years bringing her up alone and I...' she protested, unable to keep the bitterness from her voice.

'Yes, you have,' he spat. 'Now it's my turn.' His jaw had tightened and a pulse was vibrating in his temple. She had married him—that surely was enough? What more did he want from her? she wondered.

'She's not a toy. You've had your turn, now I can have mine,' she mocked in a sing-song childish voice, ridiculing what he had just said.

She had gone too far, but didn't realise till it was too late. He grabbed her by the shoulders, his hard fingers digging deeply into her blades. His grip was strong and punishing, and shook her hard till her head shot back to meet the angry bitterness on his face.

'Don't ever accuse me of playing with my daughter's emotions,' he ground out between clenched teeth, his voice hoarse and angry. 'I am her father, and from now on I shall be taking an active part in her life.'

Lauren's eyes flew open, staring at him as an angry flush of colour heated her face. She was filled with an incredulous rage as his words sank home, her mind spinning as she contemplated their implications.

'You can't—she doesn't even know you,' she said, her mouth hardening to a thin line.

She saw his eyes narrow and flinched at the coldness in his voice when he replied.

'She doesn't know me because of you,' he reminded her bitterly, the harsh accusation causing Lauren to drop her gaze. 'But she will know me, and the first thing she will learn is that you have your own life.'

Lauren was dumbfounded; she heard the grim determination in his voice and it frightened her.

'My life *is* her,' she flung back angrily. 'What other reason would I have for marrying you?' she spat at him with all the hatred she could muster. For a moment he said nothing. His face paled beneath his dark tan, his mouth hard and compressed, his dark eyes were full of misty shadows and his thick, almost raven hair added to the picture that he was a devil. Lauren shivered with fear as the change in him registered on her.

'You expect me to believe that,' he said quietly, 'when only a few hours ago you cried out for me?' He sneered with a supreme confidence.

Lauren hated his attitude—that he would mention the only thing that had been good between them. It obviously meant nothing to him other than satisfaction. He didn't mention love—ever, she recalled for the first time. No matter how passionate they had been last night he never once mentioned love. She felt used and abused by him, and to add insult to injury he was now mocking her unbridled response to him. She couldn't bear it; he was the only love she had ever known, and he had to cheapen it with his crude remarks. She hit back as hard as she could; she would not allow him the pleasure of knowing he gave her satisfaction.

'I've learnt a lot in ten years, Riccardo,' she taunted back, 'including how to massage the fragile ego of men such as yourself,' she goaded. 'Mitchell was the only man for me; I closed my eyes and thought of him—how else do you think I could bear the thought of your hands on me?' she told him, the conviction in her voice surprisingly accurate in view of the fact that it was all a lie; but she wanted to hurt him, to hurt him badly, and she knew she had succeeded.

'You little bitch,' he growled, pulling her roughly into his arms and kissing her with a ferocity that caused her pain. His lips crushed hers, his tongue forcing her lips apart as he kissed her deeply. It was bereft of the gentleness she had come to know. He was hard, cruel and demanding, taking her lips without any consideration for her.

He drew back, pushing her away from him with such force that she fell back on to the bed, her eyes wide with fear. She quickly pulled the sheet over herself, suddenly aware of her nakedness and his state of arousal.

'Don't flatter yourself,' he said contemptuously, watching her action with loathing.

Lauren winced at the cruel derision in his voice and stared at him, her eyes wide with fear.

'Listen, Lauren, I've already arranged for an au pair to look after Rebecca. When we arrive in Italy she will be there waiting. Get used to the idea—it is the best thing for both of you, believe me,' he informed her coolly, unaware of the pain he was causing her.

'No,' she shouted at him. 'I will not allow it...'

But he just shrugged his powerful shoulders lazily. 'It is arranged,' he stated simply as he began to dress.

Lauren stared at him; the man was a stranger, cold, aloof. He was trying to take Beccy from her, to punish her for the years he had lost.

'Riccardo,' she called as he opened the door to leave. He turned, the dark look in his eyes unfathomable. 'Please, Riccardo, don't take her from me,' she pleaded. The desperate note in her voice made him stiffen. She saw a flicker of light in his eyes, a sudden glow of love or compassion, but it was gone so quickly that she was unable to read it.

'Lauren,' he said in a resigned tone, 'she is our daughter, to love and share,' he explained simply.

'So there's no need for an au pair,' she replied, a glimmer of hope beginning to rise within her.

Riccardo shook his head resolutely. 'I have told you, it is for the best. It has been arranged.'

The tone in his voice held a finality that resounded in Lauren's ears till she could stand it no longer. How she hated him, she thought, and the depth of her feeling shone from her eyes. He saw the bitterness there, and shrugged, closing the door softly behind him.

'Bastard!' called Lauren as she flung herself back on the bed and cried and cried, hot angry tears of pain and frustration.

CHAPTER SEVEN

THE weary sense of defeat lay heavy on Lauren's shoulders as she sat at the breakfast table. She sipped her hot coffee with uninterest and pulled half-heartedly at the hot croissant. She couldn't believe it was happening; try as she might, Riccardo had closed every door. She had tried to fight back, but he had won. Lauren finally had no strength left. She knew that he would tire of them sooner or later, then she and Beccy could return to the life they had known.

She stared at him bitterly, hoping he could sense her anger. Did he realise the pain he would cause, the damage he could inflict upon his daughter when he tossed her aside? Lauren bit into her bottom lip. She was used to such rejection—expected it—but poor Beccy. She turned to look at her eager-faced daughter, who was listening with obvious rapture to whatever Riccardo was saying, and Lauren felt excluded—not that she wanted to be involved; it was best all round, she had decided, to keep as far away from Riccardo as possible.

Not that that proved possible. She had spend the two days before they left shopping, though Riccardo was convinced that far better and more suitable clothing could be purchased in Florence. However, he smiled indulgently as Lauren and Beccy went shopping while he arranged to have Lauren's house rented out. She had insisted upon that, so that she would have some measure of independence from him, and, as she was firmly convinced the marriage would not last, she and Beccy would

need somewhere to live on their return. Riccardo had
not troubled himself to argue the point, but Lauren
sensed his disapproval at her decision.

With the days safely taken care of Lauren's only
concern was for the nights; the thought of being alone
again with Riccardo filled her with dread. She had in-
sulted him badly, and felt sure he would not forget such
an insult lightly. The next two nights were to be spent
in the bridal suite before they flew out to Italy. The
bathroom door had been repaired, and Lauren kept her
eyes downcast whenever she was in the foyer, knowing
she must be an amusing source of gossip for the hotel
staff.

The night following their marriage, Lauren had re-
tired early and waited with increasing impatience for
Riccardo. He seemed to be ages before he finally left the
book he was reading and came to bed. She was determined not to give him the satisfaction of being a wilting
flower, and she was half reclined in bed, watching him
with a cool air despite the thudding of her heart. She
must be passive, dutiful as a wife should be, she told
herself. The prospect was daunting; he was too experienced a man, too good a lover for her to remain immune
to him, yet she had to deny those feelings, shut them
out.

He stripped off with what seemed deliberate slowness,
but Lauren remained looking at him. His body was still
as strong and as supple as ever, and she wondered if he
still swam—he had been an excellent swimmer, and they
had spent many an hour in the family's pool. Her eyes
went misty as she thought about it, happier days that
seemed so long ago.

Riccardo saw the look in her eyes, and misread her
thoughts.

'Sorry it isn't Mitchell climbing into your bed,' he growled, seeing the gentle look on her face that made him long for her till he ached.

Lauren immediately snapped out of her reverie and looked at him; it seemed pointless to antagonise him further, so she remained silent. She wished she had never said that now, but the damage was done. She felt the weight of his body on the bed, and closed her eyes. He lay on top of her immediately, his body hard and long.

'Open your eyes, Lauren,' he growled in a low, deep voice that made desire rise in her.

Her eyes shot open, and she looked directly at him; the burning need in his eyes was marred by the anger and hate that she also saw quite clearly.

'You can think of Mitchell as much as you like, whenever you like, but when we are in bed you see me— only me,' he spat out contemptuously, then, without a kiss or caress, in a brutal silence, took her.

She lay stiff, hurt and angry as he left the bed and went back to his book. Not a word was spoken between them; there were no words left to say. She had tried to pretend it wasn't happening, that in a moment he would change and become the lover she had known, but it was all over so quickly, and Lauren was left feeling totally bewildered. She did not feel she had fulfilled any duty, nor given him any satisfaction. He had left the bed with a dark, thunderous look on his face, and the wall between them rose even higher.

He had taken her, and Lauren knew she was partly to blame—had she not goaded him with her lies about Mitchell?—but it was too late now. She could never tell him the truth; she would not give him the satisfaction of knowing he was her only lover, and she doubted he would believe her word anyway. She felt outraged and alone, and hot, salty, silent tears splashed down her face, wetting the pillow.

Soon the tears of regret and sorrow were replaced with anger. Lauren was not the girl he had known—she was a woman; too many times in her life she had silently accepted whatever happened to her, but not now, she thought, suddenly outraged. She was determined that he would never, ever take her like that again. She would face him with his disgraceful behaviour, show him that she would not be party to such a practice—and it was with this final conviction that Lauren fell into a peaceful sleep.

It was several hours later before Riccardo could face her; the weight of guilt and remorse hung heavily on his shoulders, and he longed to have her forgiveness.

'Lauren,' he whispered, noting the light was still on and presuming she was still awake. She didn't move, his voice unable to penetrate the deep warmth of her loving dreams. 'Lauren,' he began again, drawing closer and stroking the stray blonde hair from her face.

She stirred slightly in her sleep, the image of Riccardo drifting before her eyes. She half smiled, still sleepy, and whispered huskily, as her arm went up to draw him close, 'Riccardo.' Then her eyes gently closed again and she sank back to the comfort of her dreams.

Riccardo stared at her, his dark eyes unreadable, and he shook his head with a sigh. Lauren stirred as he climbed into bed beside her, and she moved instinctively towards him, unaware of her body's betrayal. Her night-dress moved seductively against her skin and the deep-cut neckline exposed the fullness of her breasts. She fell against his chest and Riccardo frowned as he wrapped a protective arm around her and fell asleep.

He left the bed before she awoke, kissing her lightly on the forehead. Today they were going home, and he was in an excellent mood. He longed to show his daughter the beauty of his home; she would see it, like Lauren, for the first time with him, and the idea made him so happy.

There was a coolness between them for the whole of the journey. Riccardo had meant to apologise immediately, but there was so much to do, and as time went on it seemed unnecessary; perhaps if he were to mention it the day would be spoilt, and he wanted everything to be just right.

A car met them at the airport to drive them to the Valdi home. Lauren's heart was thudding violently against her chest as the memories came flooding back with a clarity that frightened her. Florence seemed unchanged; it held its old grandeur with fine distinction. The red-tiled Tuscan roofs blazed against the clear blue sky and the cute little drains that seemed to be topped with a steel cap still clung to every house.

It was lovely to glimpse Florence again, the Ponte Vecchio, the Baptistry, the numerous churches; Lauren's heart leapt with anticipation. All those years ago she had come here as an art student, wanting to soak up the beauty and history of the place, to see the marvellous paintings and hopefully strive for a similar skill. Though Lauren knew she was no genius, she was determined that the love she had for art would be transmitted to her pupils once she began teaching. She sighed audibly now as she thought of yet another unrealised dream.

Once the car left the city Lauren felt the familiar panic grow in the pit of her stomach. Beccy and Riccardo were far too busy talking to notice the lack of colour in her face as they drew nearer the Valdi home. Though she had met Riccardo's family at the wedding and they had seemed friendly enough, now it was different. This was their home and their true feelings could be expressed.

The car drew up outside, and Lauren's heart sank as she recalled the last time she had been here. She darted a quick look at Riccardo, but he had already grabbed Beccy's arm and was rushing for the door. She felt a stab of unhappiness; she felt surplus to requirements as usual.

Riccardo suddenly stopped and turned.

'Come on.' He smiled encouragingly, stretching out his arm to her. Lauren faltered for a moment, unsure of herself, but he beckoned her again and laughed at her. 'Come on,' he called, eager to be inside.

Lauren smiled, pushing her self-doubts away, and raced to join them. With obvious pride Riccardo wrapped his arm around both his women and marched proudly in.

The rest of the day seemed to pass in a whirl of activity. Lauren, despite her misgivings, liked the au pair; Simonetta was a plump, good-humoured girl who took an immediate liking to the pale-haired English girl who was to be her charge, and Beccy responded at once. They had spent the whole day lazing by the pool while Lauren and Riccardo talked to his family.

'I have arranged a party for tomorrow evening,' his mother explained. 'There were so many who couldn't attend the wedding, it is proper, no?' she asked Lauren, and though Lauren found it difficult to imagine there were any more family to meet she smiled sweetly as she swallowed the rising panic in her stomach.

'I've nothing really suitable to wear,' she suddenly said anxiously. She was aware of the power and wealth the

Valdi family had, and she knew a certain standard would be expected.

'Well, it is still your honeymoon; surely Riccardo will not deprive his bride of a new dress,' laughed his mother, her dark eyes dancing with unconcealed delight.

Lauren felt herself flush as Riccardo wrapped his arm around her waist and drew her close.

'I could deny her nothing, *Mamma*,' he agreed, and Lauren's pulses leapt at his admission.

'So today you rest, tomorrow you go into Firenze and you buy her a dress. Yes?' It was an instruction that was meant to be obeyed, but the warmth of her voice and the sparkle in her eyes made it seem like a suggestion.

'*Si, Mamma, prego,*' he answered like a dutiful son, and Lauren wondered, would she have the same control over her son? The thought made her colour, for it was something they had not spoken about, and she was perturbed that her own mind had travelled down such a path.

'I am going to swim before dinner, will you join me?' he asked, but Lauren shook her head. She was too confused; everything was happening so quickly, and she wasn't sure how she felt. There was something intoxicating in the air. Riccardo seemed strangely relaxed now, more like the man she had known, and the familiar surroundings were filling her mind with glorious memories.

She scolded herself grimly; one should never go back, never try to recapture one's youth and dreams of the past. She decided to read by the pool, and waved at Beccy, who was darting through the water like a mermaid, her olive-toned skin already beginning to colour.

'I hope you've put suntan lotion on,' she called, but it was Simonetta who answered.

'*Si*, madam. I see to that,' she replied confidently, and Lauren, though pleased that the girl was so responsible, felt a stab of hostility. She began to read her book, but a dark shadow fell across the pages and she looked up to face Riccardo. His dark eyes danced with devilish delight at her startled expression.

'I'm sorry—did I surprise you?' he asked, his voice faintly mocking.

'Yes, you did,' she snapped back, irritated by the effect he had on her. The close proximity of his body stirred desire deep within her.

'Still don't want to swim?' he enquired, and though the idea was tempting she refused. The water splashed with a relentless rhythm at the side of the pool. It was still hot, even though Lauren had sat in the shade, and for a moment she thought she might weaken.

'Maybe tomorrow,' she said, lowering her gaze back on her book. She couldn't help but cast a covert glance at him. His physique was marvellous, she grudgingly conceded as she watched him walk away. His lean, bronzed body was firm and hard, and Lauren felt a flush of colour stain her cheeks as she realised how vulnerable she was with him.

He walked to the edge of the pool with supreme self-assurance, and Lauren watched him as he dived skilfully into the water, barely causing a ripple on the blue surface. He then swam endless lengths, his powerful body cutting a swath through the glistening waters with obvious ease. Then he climbed from the pool with one firm push and strolled back to Lauren. He wasn't even out of breath, she noted, for some reason annoyed.

'Are you coming up to get dressed for dinner?' he asked, as he began to towel himself dry.

Lauren nodded. 'I'll just tell Beccy,' she said, rising from her chair.

'There's no need—I've given Simonetta clear instructions on Rebecca's routine,' he informed her, and Lauren felt herself bristle.

'You have, have you? And what about me? Why wasn't I consulted?' she stormed, her eyes blazing and a pain in her heart as she saw Beccy slowly being taken from her.

He shrugged his shoulders and began to make his way inside the house. Lauren followed immediately, slamming the door of their room with such force that he immediately turned, his face unreadable as he looked at her.

'She's my daughter—I expect some consideration,' she snapped at him.

'Our daughter—and what consideration did you show me?' he countered, his voice cold and unemotional. 'This is supposed to be our honeymoon; I thought we should at least try to spend some time together,' he continued, trying to explain his actions.

'Honeymoon?' she echoed, the scorn in her voice and derision in her face alerting him immediately.

He stiffened; his hair was wet and slicked smoothly off his face, revealing his cold, chiselled features, sharp and unrelenting.

'Honeymoon? After your behaviour last night you still have the nerve to mention a honeymoon?' she ridiculed with contempt.

He came towards her with a threat in his every movement, but Lauren was determined to face him squarely on this point; her own dignity was at stake.

'I will not be treated like that, Riccardo, understand that now. This marriage has been arranged for the sake of our daughter. I am aware there is no love between us, but I think we both should have enough respect for each other not to...'

She was still furious, but his eyes were boring into her with such intensity that she found it hard to continue. Any anger he had had at her words seemed to have died at her tirade. He came closer to her, taking her hand gently into his and raising it to his mouth, the kiss he so delicately gave her causing a searing heat through her body.

'You are right, of course, and I beg your forgiveness.'

His voice was low and held a smoky warmth, and he sounded truly contrite.

Lauren was dumbfounded for a moment, and stared at him in disbelief as she waited for the sting in the tail.

'In future, Lauren, I shall come as your lover or not at all,' he said crisply, and Lauren wondered what this meant. Did he truly have respect for her or, now he was back home on familiar territory, would there be many women willing to take him as a lover? Would he ever come to her again? she thought, suddenly unaccountably miserable.

She dressed for dinner with care; she still felt as if she was on probation, and she was determined to make a good impression.

There was only immediate family for dinner, and they spoke rapid Italian, constantly interrupting one another and seemingly all talking at the same time. Lauren tried to follow the conversation but she could only catch snatches, and as she had been travelling most of the day she was quite happy to let the conversation drift on around her. After dinner they all sat on the patio outside; their hill-top view looked down on the city of Florence. It was easy to pick out Brunelleschi's dome among the brown-washed buildings and Giotto's tower was clearly defined. The deep blue sky edged with scarlet held the promise of a fine day tomorrow, and Lauren longed to go, to walk around the city soaking up the atmosphere that was uniquely Florence.

A cool breeze drifted around them, bringing the heavy scent of lemons; several adorned the patio in huge terracotta tubs. Out in the fields one could hear the shrill calls of the cicadas echoing all around, and Lauren closed her eyes; the fine wine at dinner had helped her to relax and sleep began to beckon her.

'I think it is time we went to bed.' She heard Riccardo's words pierce her consciousness, but it was the cool, firm touch of his hand on hers that alerted her body. She was flustered for a moment, aware that everyone was looking at her in amusement. She tried to smile back but the smile froze on her lips as she recalled her earlier fiery words to Riccardo. She darted a look at him and he gave her a slow, slumberous smile back; the invitation he was making was clear for all to see, and Lauren felt herself blush scarlet as his family began to laugh.

He led her up the stairs, and her legs suddenly seemed leaden, unwilling to reach their room. She knew she was being silly, and tried to suffocate the alarm that was growing inside her as they approached the room.

She stopped.

'I should like to check on Beccy,' she said, which was true.

He nodded and asked, 'May I?' There was a plea in his voice that she could not ignore. She wanted to say no, to put as much distance as she could between them for as long as possible, but she knew she could not. So silently they both crept into Beccy's room. The windows were open but the shutters were closed, and the stripes of moonlight fell across her bed.

She was sound asleep, totally at peace. Unaccustomed to the heat, she had flung the sheet off the bed. Her body lay sprawled out, her pillow tossed on to the floor. Lauren bent down and put it back on the bed while Riccardo lifted her head and settled it gently back on the pillow. He picked up the discarded sheet, shaking imagined dirt from it.

Lauren watched with a painful lump growing in her throat as he lifted the sheet and laid it across their daughter's small frame with such care, tucking the sheet around her tiny shoulders. He kissed her forehead lightly and then lifted his head to Lauren. The look of tenderness in his eyes and the gentle smile on his face made her tremble. He loved their daughter; the simple fact was apparent in his every gesture and the softness of his eyes.

'She is so beautiful,' he whispered, and Lauren nodded in reply, unable to speak. He wrapped his arm around her shoulders and they both stared at the tiny figure on the bed, an angel bathed in moonlight, and so much a part of them both.

'Come,' whispered Riccardo in a low voice, as if to speak any louder would shatter the tender moment they had both shared.

He closed the door silently and they went to their own room. Lauren prepared for bed quickly, choosing the lightest of cotton slips—the night was too close for anything else. She would have preferred to sleep naked, but she lacked the confidence, and wondered what Riccardo would make of it. She snuggled down in the bed; it was cold and crisp, the sheets stiff with starch, and she waited, her heart thudding till its beat resounded in her head.

Fortunately she did not have to wait long before he joined her, though she doubted she would have fallen asleep; every nerve in her body seemed to be awake, craving attention.

He came to her softly, pulling back the covers with a slow grace that made her painfully aware of him. He slid into the bed beside her but remained silent; he turned the light out and Lauren was grateful for the blanket of darkness—she could hide her secrets in its blackness. In spite of all her courage and her firm conviction that she was right to tell him about his behaviour, she suddenly no longer felt that brave, and the silence in the room only added to the menace. She began to tremble, her body shaking uncontrollably. She tried to stop it, but her limbs shook and all attempts to pacify them failed.

He moved suddenly with the lithe grace of a panther and pulled her body towards him with a firm but gentle embrace. He rocked her as he stroked her tumbled hair from her face. The warmth of his body and the gentle rhythm soothed her trembling frame, and slowly she began to relax next to him. She turned her face to him and he kissed her. It was a tender, searching kiss, and Lauren felt herself drown in the wondrous depths of his gentleness.

He reached out his fingertips, just touching her with a gentle brush, but she quivered in response, unable and unwilling to move from his touch. She was aching for his love, and she moved closer to him till her swollen breasts met the hardness of his chest. There was a dull ache in her stomach, and she moaned softly as his hands stroked the length of her body with an expertise that made her fully attentive to his every move. He was so slow and gentle, so very, very careful that it was like a pleasurable torment, and Lauren desperately sought release.

Time seemed to become elusive as their bodies became joined as one. He kissed her passionately, allowing his teeth to sink into her arched throat as he pressed down on her. Her body shook with the intensity of feeling and quivered with delight as he sank down beside her and drew her still closer to him. She snuggled against his chest and tried in vain to stay awake, to prolong this moment of pleasure, for she knew that despite everything she loved him and longed for his love in return. She knew she could never have that, that he would never forgive her, and she also knew that rejection for her was never far away.

It was just before dawn when Riccardo awoke. Lauren was still lying across him, her sheet of wheaten hair falling across his shoulders and chest. For a while he lay quite still, looking down at her, remembering last night and thinking of all she had been through.

Finally he eased her from his chest and slipped from the bed. She looked so peaceful, so defenceless. Swiftly he bent down and kissed her soft lips, then he turned and left.

It was some time later before Lauren awoke to her cold empty bed. The joy of last night and the love she had felt in his tenderness vanished as quickly as the morning dew. She could arouse him, together their bodies responded to one another, but there was to be nothing else between them. The gap was far too wide to bridge, she though miserably, and sighed. Today they were going to Florence, and nothing was going to prevent her from having a marvellous time. Pushing all thoughts to the back of her mind, she hurried to get ready.

'At last—I thought you would have preferred an earlier start,' chastised Riccardo as he lowered his paper to look at her. He was sitting on the patio under the twisting vines of grapes. 'Coffee?' he offered, pouring a fresh cup of espresso from the jug. Lauren smiled and sipped the dark brew, suddenly feeling self-conscious.

'You should have woken me. It was the travelling—it always makes me tired,' she confessed, then caught the look of amusement in his eyes and lowered her head.

The day was perfect—the sun was still not too hot and a gentle cool breeze freshened the air. They decided to walk down, as parking in Florence was a nightmare. Lauren had no desire to go in any museum or art gallery today; she wanted to stroll around to rekindle old memories. They passed the bronze statue of Il Porcellino, and Lauren reached out and touched its snout.

'You know the story?' he asked, watching her action.

'Hans Christian Andersen's tale,' she admitted, knowing by the look of scorn on his face that that was not the one he meant.

'No, we have our own tale; after dark this ugly boar was able to transform himself into a man as "beautiful as Saint Sebastian newly painted". He fell in love with a lovely young girl and begged her to keep his secret, otherwise he would be fixed in bronze forever. She, like most women...' He paused to laugh at the look of outrage on Lauren's face when he criticised her sex. 'She could not keep a secret, and told her mother. By nightfall the whole of Florence knew, and he has remained a bronze statue ever since.'

He laughed as he linked his arm through hers. She looked at him and thought how apt the tale was; she had a lover by night but a master by day.

It was a short walk through the narrow streets before they reached the select shopping area. Lauren knew there would be no point in arguing as the Valdi name was at stake; here, she knew, she must look her best. She paused at the door to an exclusive boutique, her eyes glancing at the name ornately scrolled in gold across the frontage. She swallowed nervously, glancing at Riccardo for support.

He smiled. 'Francesca is an old friend of mine; it is no problem.'

This did nothing to alleviate Lauren's misgivings; in fact she felt a stab of hostility towards her unknown rival. She had no need; Francesca was not the young woman she had suspected. She was a slender woman in her late fifties, but despite her age she was extremely attractive. Her clothes fitted her to perfection—the colours and style seemed to be made for her.

'Ricci!' she screeched the moment she saw him, and she flung her arms about him; they exchanged hugs enthusiastically.

'My wife,' he said, the pride in his voice evident, and Lauren felt her cheeks colour. She was stunned when she was greeted in the same affectionate way, and tried to respond despite her natural English reserve.

'You wish for me to dress her, no?' Francesca asked as she produced a tape measure from nowhere.

Riccardo nodded.

'Of course, but we have no time—the dress must be ready for this evening; she is to be formally introduced,' he explained.

Lauren turned, her eyes wide with fear; the idea she had of a family gathering was suddenly taking on a different complexion.

'Formal?' she queried, the element of alarm in her voice.

Riccardo smiled and shrugged his powerful shoulders as he held out his hands, palm upwards. He shook his head from side to side.

'It is a chance for you to be introduced to the families of Florence,' he explained, trying to make it sound far less daunting than it was.

'I thought you just meant your family,' she persisted as the panic about her evening ahead filled her troubled mind.

'It is of no matter,' intervened Francesca in a conciliatory tone. 'You will be the envy of every woman— you are an English beauty in your own right, and you have captured one of Florence's leading men.'

Captured was the right expression, thought Lauren glumly; she had trapped him by bearing his child, and yet it was she who felt the true captive, alone in an alien environment.

She looked at the endless rows of dresses; the choice was too daunting to make, and she had no idea where to begin. She had never in her life spent that much on a year's clothes, never mind one dress. She felt for sure that no matter how beautiful it was she could never wear it in Florence again. It would be an insult to the Valdi wealth.

Lauren sank down on to the white wicker chair and waited for Francesca to bring her some clothes. The array of designs quite stunned her, but they all seemed far too sophisticated for her, and she felt sure she would feel self-conscious dressed in such finery.

Riccardo nodded his head and smiled appreciatively as Francesca hurried back and forth, seeking something that would meet with his approval. But there seemed to be nothing suitable—Lauren's pale colouring would have been swamped by the rich vibrancy of most of Francesca's designs.

'I have something, Riccardo; it is not so expensive,' she said apologetically, 'but I think it will suit the *signora*.'

She scurried away and returned moments later with the garment. Lauren knew immediately that the dress was the one for her. Its simplicity and pale light blue colour would suit her, she was sure.

Riccardo viewed the simple cut with a frown and fingered the fine silk fabric with discernment.

'Put it on,' he instructed Lauren, and she darted away to the cubicles at the back, ignoring for once his arrogant attitude. Francesca was more than helpful; she carefully helped Lauren to dress. The neckline was a simple scallop but it was heavy with sequins and beading in a thick, intricate design. It gave the dress a sophistication without taking away the beauty of the cut, and it fitted beautifully, falling around Lauren's curves, adding a seductive shape to her figure. The back of the dress was cut in a dramatic deep V, giving her a more sexy image than she was used to.

'Come, show him,' encouraged Francesca, but Lauren shook her head.

'No, it's my decision, I shall have it.' She saw the troubled look on Francesca's face and patted her hand reassuringly. 'It will be a surprise. It does suit me, doesn't it?' she asked, suddenly anxious.

Francesca beamed with delight. '*Si*, it is made for you, no?'

Lauren nodded, her mind already in a whirl about the rest of her evening wear—shoes, for instance, and her hair, she thought, would certainly have to be put up to achieve the full effect of the dress.

Riccardo's frown deepened when she returned not wearing the dress.

'Well, where is it?' he demanded.

'I've decided to have it—Francesca is wrapping it at the moment,' she answered with a secret smile on her lips.

He looked at her quizzically. 'Surely I should see it first, give my opinion.'

There was a tone of indignation in his voice that made Lauren giggle, and he looked at her in surprise.

'There is a joke?' he asked seriously.

'I'm not a child; I choose my own clothes, and I know you will be pleased with the result,' she retorted, grinning at him, suddenly feeling she had an upper hand at last.

'You had better be the best dressed woman there,' he reminded her coldly, hoping her amusement would evaporate.

He was wrong.

'But of course, Riccardo, but first there are one or two other things I must buy.' She grinned wickedly, taking the parcel from Francesca and making for the door.

He shrugged his powerful shoulders in a gesture of defeat and smiled to himself. It pleased him to see her so confident. He caught up with her, taking the parcel and linking his arm through hers.

'Be careful, Lauren,' he warned her quietly, enjoying the banter between them. 'You're beginning to sound like a real wife.'

Lauren smiled back but felt a stab of pain; she could never be a real wife because she knew she would never have his love, but she was determined to make him proud of her this evening.

'Would you like to have a coffee with me?' he asked, waiting for her reaction. Lauren looked at him and smiled.

'I thought you'd never ask,' she said, her eyes darting around looking for a empty café.

'No, no, not here,' he said hurriedly as he drew her away from the major streets.

Lauren gave a gasp when she realised where she was, and he flashed a look at her.

'You remember?' he asked, and she nodded. How could she forget? It was the cheapest place in town, always full of boisterous students. It was here they had first met; it seemed like an eternity ago.

'Oh, Riccardo,' she said simply, her eyes filling with tears as he went to the very same table and drew out the chair she had sat on all those years ago.

'Are we Italians not famed for our romance?' he laughed as she sat down. 'Today, though, there is a difference—we shall each have some cake. No need to share one slice,' he joked, and Lauren laughed freely. She had never been so happy in all her life.

CHAPTER EIGHT

LAUREN could have stayed in that tiny little café all day, but she had to finish her shopping. The shopkeepers in Florence were as keen as any other Italians on their siestas—it was considered sacrosanct, so it was imperative that Lauren finish her shopping before noon.

Shoes were no problem as the selection was endless; finally she chose a pair of slim pale blue shoes decorated with a buckle in silver. She was determined to dress her hair, and insisted that Riccardo wait at a bar while she bought what she needed so that the finished effect would be a complete surprise.

'I would like to buy you something,' Riccardo offered as she approached, laden down with an assortment of bags.

For a moment she was going to protest, but she saw the flash of disappointment in his eyes and smiled instead.

'That's very kind of you, but surely you have brought me enough?' she laughed, holding the bags high in the air.

'One more gift,' he said, taking her up through the streets to the Ponte Vecchio.

The whole bridge was lined with goldsmiths and silversmiths, each one specialising in its own designs. Riccardo knew exactly where he was going, and took Lauren into a tiny workshop. There, after much deliberation, he chose for her a fine piece of jewellery. It was a thin coiled twist of several colours, just enough to enhance the dress without detracting from it in any way. Lauren took the box, and her heart leapt at the romanticism.

But Riccardo shattered her illusions at once.

'Wear it tonight—it will be expected,' he informed her, unaware of the pain in her eyes.

Once the shopping was finished Lauren could hardly wait to return to the villa. She had not forgotten Beccy, and had bought her a very fashionable outfit. She was delighted with all her purchases, and she walked with a brisk step, suddenly feeling very happy.

Riccardo watched her with interest, his chocolate-brown eyes warm and soft as he saw the girl he had known ten years ago.

Lauren waited with increasing impatience for Riccardo to leave their room. She still had some misgivings about the party; she would rather it had been smaller, less grand. Crowds bothered her, made her feel even more insignificant.

She dressed with care, applying a little make-up with a delicate touch but emphasising her pale eyes with plenty of dark mascara. She lowered her head, brushing her hair till it fell like a golden sheaf on to her lap, then, with considerable skill, she twisted and turned it. Finally she raised herself up again to clip her hair in place.

The transformation was astounding. The added height her new hairstyle gave her made her look regal and self-assured. She placed the *diamanté* clips she had chosen just above each ear so that they would catch the light whenever she moved her head. She then stepped into the dress. Her heart was already racing and her legs trembled a little as she stepped with care into its gentle folds. She drew the dress up along her shapely legs, enjoying the soft feel of the silk against her body. The zip was neatly concealed at the side, giving the impression that the dress was almost a second skin. Lauren was surprised at the weight of the sequinned neckline, and patted it self-consciously as she turned slowly and she looked in the full-length mirror.

She gave a slow smile of satisfaction—it was hard not to. She would have had difficulty recognising herself, she admitted. She slipped her feet into her shoes and sprayed herself with some perfume. She was ready now but the prospect of meeting all those people was still daunting.

Lauren took a long deep breath several times before she felt confident enough to open the bedroom door. She could hear the band playing, its beat travelling on the night air. The buzz of conversation, typical Italian— loud and fast and constantly punctuated with laughter— seemed to fill the air. She paused, suddenly frightened, then suffocated her feelings, stiffened her back and began a slow descent.

Riccardo was waiting at the foot of the stairs. He turned as he heard her approach, and the joy that poured into Lauren's heart was unimaginable. He looked, turned away, then, as the realisation hit him, he turned again. His eyes sparkled as he raised his hand to take hers and drew her down towards him, wrapping his arm around her waist while he whispered in her ear.

'You look marvellous.' His voice was husky and full of pride.

'Do I?' she breathed, her head spinning with excitement in the knowledge that she had pleased him. The firm grip around her slim waist was confirmation enough, and he swept her into the huge hall, eager to present his wife.

Lauren faltered as they entered; the room was full to capacity, and the noise seemed to race through her ears. The applause that broke out as they walked in was deafening, and Lauren felt her face colour with embarrassment. She hadn't expected such a response. Then she had to wait at Riccardo's side while numerous people came to offer their congratulations. She was grateful to him; he seemed to want this part of the evening over as quickly as she, and he was polite but very brief. The row of strangers passed before her without anyone's name registering. Then Lauren saw a familiar face from the past, and she smiled warmly as Maria approached. She had been surprised that she had not already visited—there was a time when she had never been away from the Valdi home.

'Congratulations,' Maria purred, viewing Lauren coldly. 'Better late than never, I suppose.' She laughed lightly, but Lauren failed to see the humour and flushed scarlet, her eyes darting around the room, fearful that someone would hear her. Unfortunately most had, and a trickle of laughter spread around the room. Lauren was horrified, and her embarrassment was compounded when Riccardo said something in rapid Italian which caused even more laughter. She had no idea what he had said—it had been spoken too quickly amid much laughter—but she caught her name and knew she was part of the joke.

She glared at Riccardo, but he was too busy laughing to notice the look of outrage on her face. It was spoilt for her—the whole evening ruined. She wanted to talk to Maria, to thank her for her past help, but she left almost immediately.

Lauren felt so alone; she felt she had become the butt of everyone's joke, and withdrew. She sat silently most of the evening, sipping the expensive wine with little interest. Riccardo made several attempts to cajole her into joining in the fun, but she was in no mood; the evening seemed to drag on relentlessly.

'Lauren,' he whispered fiercely through clenched teeth, giving the impression he was smiling. 'For God's sake, what's wrong now?'

'Nothing,' she snapped back, knowing it was pointless to explain; he just wouldn't understand.

He pulled her to her feet, the cold look in his dark eyes making her gasp.

'Then stop sulking like a schoolgirl and join the party. It is in our honour,' he reminded her as he drew her on to the dance-floor.

The crowd parted, allowing them to dance freely, and Lauren immediately stiffened, becoming like a board under the gaze of so many people. Riccardo held her even closer, his hard cheek resting on her face and his lips touching her ear with a delicacy that sent a shiver of delight through her body.

'Relax,' he murmured, his tongue playing with her ear till she melted against him. Her heart thudded violently and she wished her dress had been higher at the back. His hands seemed to press against her naked flesh, searing her with their heat.

They danced slowly across the floor, their bodies moving as one with the sound of the music. Soon other dancers joined them, and Lauren felt it was time she left the dance-floor. She could not trust her body so close next to Riccardo's. She tried to move away from him but he refused to let her. Sharply he pulled the lower half of her body against his hard limbs until she was aware of every muscle of him. She knew her heart was pounding as she felt his body harden with desire.

'Riccardo,' she protested, alarmed by his behaviour in view of so many people. Her cheeks began to burn as he deliberately teased her. She was convinced that everyone was watching, and was mortified at his outrageous conduct. She was grateful when she was finally excused by a portly gentleman whose dancing skills were questionable but whose manners, unlike Riccardo's, were impeccable.

The night was long and laborious for Lauren; she felt as if every whisper was about her. She knew the wedding had come as a shock to most people—including her, she thought ruefully. Then, with the addition of a ten-year-old child, she was sure the gossips must be having a field day.

It was well past midnight before the final guests left. Lauren was exhausted and emotionally in tatters. She had felt completely out of her depth and had still not recovered from Maria's remark. It seemed so odd that Maria of all people had treated her unkindly. She had always been there in the past. Indeed, sometimes Riccardo had grown irritated by her constant companionship. Now she seemed to view Lauren as an enemy and she certainly did not stay at the house so often.

Lauren had hoped that Riccardo would defend her—perhaps she would have felt better then—but instead he had joined in, making her a joke and laughing-stock among all his friends.

Lauren undressed uninterestedly, tossing her expensive gown with contempt to the floor. Riccardo watched her action, his dark eyes narrowing briefly, but he remained silent. When she flopped into bed, tired and unhappy, Riccardo was at her side within moments, and she immediately turned away from him, an angry wall of silence building up between them.

'What's wrong now?' he snapped, sitting up and snapping the light back on.

She turned, outraged that he could ask such a question; was he so insensitive to her needs?

'I just don't like being the butt of your jokes,' she bit back at him, her eyes flashing icily at his cool expression.

He frowned, viewing her with a sudden spark of anger.

'I've no idea what you're talking about,' he informed her with a menace in his voice that should have warned her to be silent.

'Haven't you?'

'No, I haven't; perhaps you could explain?' he mocked in a low voice.

'You and Maria seemed to have a good laugh at my expense—you and everyone else who was there this evening,' she retorted, her face blazing as she recalled the incident. The laughter still seemed to ring in her ears.

'Stop over-reacting, Lauren, it was a bit of fun among friends—that's family life,' he explained.

Lauren swallowed the pain in her heart as she looked at him.

'How dare you mention family life to me? You know what my life was like, yet you throw it in my face at the first opportunity,' she shouted.

Riccardo was furious; the gleam in his eyes darkened dangerously and he glowered at her with unconcealed contempt.

'That's not what I mean, and you know it. Grow up, Lauren; it's past and gone. How much longer are you going to allow your past to ruin our future?' he continued forcibly.

'Future? We have no future, and only a fool would think we had,' she said coldly, suddenly aware of the distance between them.

He didn't waste his breath on a reply but flung her back on to the bed, crushing her with his weight. She hated him and hated herself even more as a sea of desire spread through her because of his close proximity. For a moment they lay there, totally aware of each other.

'Is this it?' mocked Lauren. 'Is this all we have?' she taunted him, fixing her ice-blue eyes on his dark orbs, locked in battle.

'Shut up,' he replied savagely, his breath sharp and rasping. 'I don't want to hear any more. Talking to you is a waste of breath. This is all you seem to want from me—all you understand.'

Lauren gave a gasp as she tried to move away, but he pulled the covers from her and trapped her with hard, cruel hands. She began to struggle but his mouth was hard and uncompromising; he was determined to win, to force her compliance.

She began to tremble, shuddering under the weight of his hard body and the deep probing of his harsh lips hungrily devouring hers. Lauren had ceased to try and fight him; her battle now was with herself. She had to control the seeping desire that was coursing through her veins, for despite everything she ached for him.

'Riccardo, listen, this isn't the answer, you know that,' she whispered huskily as his hands descended on her yielding body.

'No.' His brown eyes mocked her as he lowered his head to her exposed body. 'I'm tired of listening to your voice when your body tells me quite a different story.'

The derision in his voice was reflected in the firm strokes of his hands as he explored her body. His hands were harder than usual, his touch rough and hungry with desire, and the effect on Lauren was electrifying. She felt as if she was spinning in the dark depths of her very being, and yet she felt so completely at one with him.

His mouth forced her tender lips apart; his hardness was bruising and his kiss contemptuous. With masterful strokes he slid his possessive hand around her breast, cupping it in a harsh, angry grip till Lauren gave a cry of pain and pleasure. Lauren was no longer resisting his onslaught; she moaned as her defences melted with every touch he made, her body quivering with anticipation as the darkness of his hard body was suddenly on top of her. She automatically became soft and pliant, his hands resting on either side of her head, his knees parting her thighs with ease.

For a moment Lauren stiffened, aware of his anger and the force and strength of the man. Tightly she wound her arms around his neck, pulling him down on her. The heavy gasps of his panting echoed in her ears, renewing her own passion, and she cried his name as her body shook with convulsive spasms.

Afterwards they both lay in silence, a cold, angry silence that was bereft of any love. She heard him get up and leave the bed, but she squashed the desire to call his name and allowed herself tears only when she heard the bedroom door close.

Sleep was elusive; Lauren's mind buzzed with the night's events. She was troubled. Did she live in the past so much that she denied herself a future? Had she robbed Beccy of a loving father because of her own fears of commitment? She tossed and turned, vividly remembering herself as a lonely child and the brutal man who was her father.

Sleep finally came, and Lauren slept with surprising composure, awakening feeling refreshed, her mind still whirling with Riccardo's accusation and a determi-

nation to face the truth. He had not returned to spend
the night with her, and Lauren felt a stab of unhappiness. Had she finally driven him away?

Then a cold reality swept over her and she leapt from
the bed, grabbing her gown and calling Beccy's name as
she flew down the corridor, her heart thudding painfully
against her chest. She flung open Beccy's door; her room
was silent and empty. Lauren knew immediately what
had happened; she rushed back to her own room,
dressing with extreme speed and rushing from the house.
She had no idea where to look; the idea was too painful
to contemplate, but the reality of her missing child was
a fact. She felt at a loss; she would get no help from the
police, she knew that, and her heart sank at the desperate situation she was in.

She walked up and down aimlessly, leaving the city of
Florence without being aware of it. She wandered outside
the city walls, her mind numb with grief. She had no
idea how far or long she had been walking—time seemed
to hang heavy on her heart. She had lost her daughter
despite everything, and the anguish was unbearable.
Would Riccardo allow her visiting rights or would Beccy
just disappear the way so many children did in custody
battles?

The sun was high in the sky, and thirst and aching
feet forced Lauren into a shady bar. She dug deep into
her jeans pocket, retrieving enough money for an ice-
cool lemonade. She sighed wearily as she sank on to the
chair and closed her eyes against the glare of the sunshine. The sweet smell of fresh basil filled the air, and
enticing aromas of country food assailed her nostrils.
She suddenly felt hungry, and a young Italian waiter appeared almost immediately at her side. His dark hair
was thick and unruly and his face youthful—remi-

niscent of how Riccardo used to look, Lauren thought as she smiled at the young man.

'Diego,' he said, offering her a handwritten menu all in Italian.

'*Grazie*,' Lauren nodded, taking the card and flicking through it, looking for the cheapest dish. She ordered a pizza square, and was delighted by the enormous size of it. It was plain pizza and it bore no relation to the factory-made ones in England. The base was thick and soft, cooked in an open oven—this one's being wood-burning added to its natural flavour. The tomato sauce was fresh, teeming with garlic and fresh basil, and the cheese on top was melting underneath several thin slices of spicy salami.

Lauren sank her teeth into the hot pizza, pulling back to snap the long strands of cheese. It was delicious, and Diego, who stood waiting for her approval, smiled glee-fully at her enjoyment. When he returned with her drink he sat down with her. Lauren was feeling a little better, and she sat back, sipping her drink and politely answering Diego's questions. He was friendly, and they talked; he told her some silly story, and Lauren started to laugh.

She hadn't noticed the car draw up or heard the angry slamming of a car door. The first thing she knew of Riccardo's arrival was the sudden clatter of chairs hitting the ground as he tossed them out of his way and made purposefully towards her, cutting a swath between the tables and chairs. Anger was stamped on every line of his face and a cold smile curved his lips.

Diego, sensing trouble, protested at first, but Riccardo's dark eyes snapped at him.

'This is my husband...' began Lauren weakly, trying to defuse the situation; but it was pointless. Riccardo glared at her and her heart leapt with fear. She immediately became silent, her pulse racing as he drew closer. He grabbed her wrist with such force that she could feel his fingers digging painfully into her wrist. He dragged her to her feet, the table crashing to the floor as he pulled her towards him with such force that she fell heavily against his chest, forcing the breath from her.

'Lauren.' His voice was brusque and his fingers punitive as he led her back to the car. Lauren did not even dare to protest; she had never seen him so furious before, and suddenly, for the first time, she saw his true Latin temperament, and it frightened her. She swallowed nervously as he pulled open the car door and pushed her inside with all his might. She fell heavily against the steering-wheel but immediately pulled herself straight, snapping the seatbelt around herself as a form of barrier. He marched round the car, his face grim, his eyes as black as night, and the storm that swirled within them had not broken yet.

Lauren sat as still as could be, not wanting to feel his wrath but knowing it was inevitable. The car roared to life, his foot heavy on the accelerator, and he thrust it into gear with a force that made Lauren shudder. He looked extremely attractive, driving his car with such a devilish air, and Lauren hated the feeling of excitement he was arousing in her. The drive back to the house was fast, but she was still surprised by the amount of ground she had covered. She looked at her watch and gave a gasp; she had not realised it was so late. She had been away from the house all morning, and now it was late afternoon.

She darted a look at Riccardo's face; the tension was chiselled deep into his hard features. He drew up outside and Lauren climbed from the car with shaky legs; her heart was racing and her pulses leapt as she followed him into the house.

The silence that surrounded them thudded against her ears; they were obviously alone, and the thought terrified her. She could sense his anger, but the stillness disturbed her even more. Where was Beccy?

She stopped immediately, no longer following him like an errant child; she was blazing with anger at the arrogance of the man. She was only putting up with him for the sake of her daughter.

'Where is she?' she spat at him, the harsh, angry contempt apparent in her glacial tone. He spun on his heels to face her, and they stood locked in an immobile anger that froze them. His dark eyes flicked to hers, brooding and unfathomable, and a frown creased his brow. He raked his strong tapering fingers through his hair, pushing his thick black locks from his face, and glared at her.

'Where's who?' he snapped back, equally angry, his black head turning with chilling slowness.

Lauren's temper boiled over and she flushed hotly, her hands twisting in angry confusion, guilt and frustration written on her troubled face. She did not want to play this cat-and-mouse game. He had her child. Had taken her and was now dangling her like a toy before her eyes, so that he could force her to become what he wanted. A docile female who would accept anything he handed out. She was incensed; all the pent-up frustrations she had ever felt against men, all the built-up hatred for her father, all the anger and bitterness of an innocent child unable to fight back increased her anger.

'Where is she ... ?' she began again, trying to keep the spiralling panic she felt safely under control.

'You mean Beccy, don't you?' he demanded. His jaw clamped together and his voice hardened still further as he went on, 'You think I've taken Beccy.'

Lauren stared at him, her eyes flashing, hating him bitterly for playing with her like this.

'I want her back,' she stated simply, not wanting to sound too demanding but to sound in control despite the turmoil of emotions.

'You really think I've taken her?' he asked again, his voice hoarse with anger, and his eyes leapt with temper as he tried to control it.

Lauren stared at him, her eyes wide with fear as she saw the darkening storm on his face. He wanted to hurt her by depriving her of Beccy. She nodded numbly, unable to face the look of accusation in his eyes, yet she knew she was right. Beccy certainly wasn't here.

'Haven't you taken Beccy?' she snapped, keeping her head lowered, half praying that he was telling the truth, that Beccy was safe.

'No,' was his emphatic answer as he pinned her arms to her sides. 'What makes you think I would take her?' he growled. '*Why* would I?' he insisted, his dark eyes boring into hers till she could take it no longer.

'Because you want her; you married me because you want her,' she cried back at him, hurt and angry, hating to have to admit that simple truth.

'I haven't taken her, Lauren, she has gone shopping with my mother,' he informed her icily, his eyes leaping with anger. 'A fact you would have been informed of had you not jumped to hasty conclusions.'

'Her room was empty and you were gone too,' Lauren explained simply, matching the look in his eyes with equal hostility and misunderstanding.

'So you presumed I'd taken her. Had the gardener not seen you rushing from the house like someone possessed I wouldn't even have known you had gone. I've been looking for you since then. I might have guessed you'd be up to your old tricks,' he spat at her bitterly.

Lauren jumped, backing away, seeing the menace in his face, the threat of unleashed anger in his stiff body. Her heart thudded painfully at her constricting chest, making her breathing painful and rapid. Riccardo stood in front of her, the strain of controlling his temper etched on his face. His hand gripped her shoulders in a vice-like hold, and Lauren winced with the pain.

'Now listen, Lauren, and understand this: you're my wife now and I expect you to behave like one. I will never take Rebecca from you, but if you are not careful you will drive us away—both of us away. Do I make myself clear?' he growled.

She stared at him, their eyes locked in combat.

'How do I know you mean that?' she asked.

'Lauren!' he roared, shaking her shoulders in anger. 'Stop it, stop it.' There was a plea in his voice that she couldn't understand, and she looked at him, puzzled.

'What do you mean? Stop what?' she asked, troubled by him.

'Stop judging me and every other man by your father. Some are worse but, believe me, most are better,' he growled at her, his eyes black with rage before marching away.

Lauren watched him walk away, his heels clicking noisily against the marble floor. She clenched and un-clenched her fists at her sides as she tried to comprehend what he had just told her.

CHAPTER NINE

LAUREN stared after him, the tension apparent in every move of his body. His strides were long and purposeful and dangerously powerful. He was so angry, and yet there seemed to be an underlying sadness, a sense of frustration. She watched him march down the long hall for a long time, her brow furrowed as he slammed the door of his office. She felt all alone; she sighed, suddenly feeling very foolish, and she climbed the stairs with a heavy heart.

It is happening again, she thought, I am destroying the faint chance of happiness I have. The long walk and argument with Riccardo had drained her, and for a moment the thought of sleep seemed delightful—till she heard Beccy's voice. She darted to her bedroom window and looked down at the extensive terraces and large pool.

Beccy was splashing around in the water, completely carefree, oblivious to the trouble she was causing. Lauren was grateful for that; she didn't want Beccy to know how much bitterness there was between her and her father, but how much longer could the pretence go on? The sun had warmed Beccy's skin even further and a deep tan was developing and her hair lightening with the sun's rays. She looks even more beautiful, Lauren thought, but there again I am her mother, she reminded herself with a smile.

She decided to join her at once; they had seen so little of each other, and she desperately wanted Beccy to be happy. She changed within moments into a one-piece swimsuit. It was plain black, but the lace-up front and high-cut legs made her look very sexy. She turned to look at herself in the mirror and was suddenly conscious of how she looked, so wrapped a thick towel from the bathroom around herself before going down to the pool. She ran outside, tossing the towel with abandonment on to a patio chair, and dived in. The water hit her body, icy cold, and she gave a cry as she disappeared underneath the waves she had created. Beccy turned as she heard the splash and swam over to her surfacing mother, grinning with delight.

'Where have you been?' she asked, a worried look on her face. 'Riccardo was really upset when he couldn't find you,' she said before swimming away.

'I just went for a walk,' supplied Lauren, swimming after her. She was annoyed that Beccy knew anything about it; was he using Beccy as a weapon against her? 'Was Riccardo annoyed with you?' she asked, trying to make her voice sound light and casual as they both leant against the side of the pool, their legs floating aimlessly.

Beccy laughed as she splashed her mother's face.

'Why should he be angry with me? It was you who went missing.'

She flooded Lauren's face with a huge wave of water before darting away. Lauren spluttered, and shook her head, swimming after Beccy with long, strong strokes. She caught her by the ankle and dragged her down, her laughter carrying as Beccy's body twisted and twirled in the water.

They were unaware they were being watched. Riccardo stood at the open window of his office, his eyes dark and brooding and his heart heavy as he saw them playing together like a pair of children, splashing and ducking each other, racing the length of the pool, helping each other to perfect their dive. They looked more like sisters than mother and daughter as they swam together. Lauren lay back, floating on the water; the sun was shining down and she was too tired to play any longer. It was fun just to drift in the water, splashing her arms now and again. Beccy had climbed from the pool and was sitting in the shade sipping an ice-cold drink.

Lauren jumped as she heard the splash, her eyes darting round anxiously, waiting to see where Beccy would pop up. Suddenly she felt someone grab her foot, and within moments she was swirling in the depths of the pool. A pair of strong arms were wound tightly around her waist and they surfaced in unison, their bodies locked together. Lauren gasped and struggled for release, but Riccardo just laughed. He was enjoying the feel of her wet body fused next to his.

Lauren coloured as she followed the direction of his gaze; her lace had become loose in the struggle and her swelling breasts were heaving against his hard chest. She could feel the strength of his muscular legs as he kicked them lightly to ensure they both stayed afloat. The water seemed to caress their bodies, relaxing them both. Lauren wriggled unsuccessfully in his tight grip, and flushed with colour as she realised the effect she was having on him. His eyes were slumberous with invitation and his voice had grown smoky.

'Lauren,' he murmured throatily as he drew her close, his warm lips claiming hers.

Lauren knew she could not fight him; her body melted at his touch. Beccy, seeing them together, joined them with a splash, swimming over to enjoy the fun. Lauren struggled even harder for release as she saw Beccy approach, and Riccardo drew back and laughed even louder.

'What's wrong, Lauren, still trying to run away?' he taunted.

'I'm tired, that's all,' she said grumpily, hating her body's betrayal whenever he was close. He released her as Beccy came up beside them.

'Let's have a race, shall we?' she asked enthusiastically, unaware of the tension between the two adults.

'I'll win,' Riccardo stated confidently, and Beccy laughed at his attitude while Lauren grimaced.

'To the end of the pool,' yelled Beccy, already swimming as fast as she could.

Riccardo laughed. 'Hey, that's not fair; you started before us,' he called after her, soon catching her up.

Lauren watched them both, so at ease with one another, so sure of their feelings. She sighed as she made her way over to the side of the pool and climbed out. She wrapped her towel around her body and glanced backwards, watching them play in the pool with a stab of jealousy.

'Hey, where's Mum going? Mum?' called Beccy, puzzled by her sudden departure.

'I think she's tired,' explained Riccardo, watching Lauren leave, his eyes dark and troubled. 'Come on, let's race again,' he laughed, catching the look of sorrow on his daughter's face and suddenly feeling angry.

Lauren went to her room, and closed the window so that she could not hear the laughter and fun Beccy and Riccardo were having with one another. The pain was too much to bear. It was obvious that he loved his daughter very much, and it hurt Lauren to know that she would never have a part of that love. She lay down on the bed and drifted off into a deep sleep, but she was tormented by visions of Riccardo running away with Beccy, and she awoke with a start when the bedroom door opened.

'What's the matter?' asked Riccardo, seeing the look of fear on her face.

'I thought you'd gone——' she began, but he cut in at once, his voice cold as steel.

'Gone with Beccy, I presume?' he growled, his eyes flashing as he glared at her. He turned on his heels and slammed out of the room. The door vibrated against the walls with a shudder, the noise preventing him from hearing her call.

Lauren sank back on to the bed, his name still hanging in the air. She had wanted to explain, to tell him it was just a dream—she understood that; but it was too late— he hadn't even waited for an explanation.

She was grateful that Beccy joined them for dinner as the atmosphere was strained despite the impeccable wines and lovely food. The silence around the table was tangible, and Beccy's eyes darted frantically from one adult to the other, but they kept their heads lowered, unable to face each other or their daughter.

'Can we go out on another picnic?' asked Beccy, troubled by the tension. Lauren's eyes darted up, warning her to be silent, and Beccy coloured when she saw the look of anger on her mother's face. Riccardo shot a look at Lauren when he saw poor Beccy looking so sad. He frowned at her, but she kept her head down, fully aware of his disapproval.

'Yes, I think that's an excellent idea—tomorrow too soon?' he joked, enjoying the look of gratitude on Beccy's face.

'No, that's great, isn't it, Mum?' she asked Lauren, who was using all her powers of concentration to dissect her fish.

'Hmm,' she agreed. 'I'll think about it,' she added, not wanting to commit herself.

Beccy pushed back her chair in anger and stood up, her small face angry and troubled.

'It's not my fault you two aren't friends,' she accused her mother, her face distorted in anger as she glared at her.

Lauren's head shot up and she stared in disbelief at her little daughter; she could see the pain so clearly etched in her innocent face, and her own heart sank.

'Beccy...' she began, her voice trembling with emotion as she reached out to touch her, but Beccy had already drawn back, her eyes sparkling in defiance.

'Don't touch me; you don't care for me, you don't care for my father, you only care for yourself. I want to go on the picnic, and I hate you, I hate——'

'Rebecca!' barked Riccardo, his voice deep and strong and his eyes staring at her in anger.

Beccy froze and turned to look at him; hot, angry tears were already forming in her eyes as she looked at him.

'Apologise to your mother at once,' he demanded, his voice stinging.

'I don't see why I sh——' Beccy began to protest, still annoyed with Lauren, but Riccardo snapped,

'Now, Rebecca,' and he laid down his napkin with a cold precision as he started to rise from his chair.

Beccy's defiance evaporated and she lowered her head.

'I'm sorry,' she mumbled in a low voice, a sullen look on her face.

'I doubt your mother can hear that, which is odd because we heard everything else you wanted to say with crystal clarity,' he reminded her, the anger in his voice even worrying Lauren. She wasn't sure how far to let Riccardo go; until that moment she had never considered there would ever be any problems with Beccy— now she wasn't so sure.

Beccy darted a look of anguish at her mother, but Lauren was too numb; all her worst fears seemed to be coming true and history was about to repeat itself. How clearly she had seen herself mirrored in her small daughter.

'I'm sorry,' said Beccy, louder, her voice heavy with sarcasm.

Riccardo glared at her, his eyes flaring with lights of anger in his deep-set eyes.

'Go to your room,' he snapped. 'We shall discuss this later.'

Beccy faltered for a minute; she was hungry, and dinner had only just begun.

'Now!' roared Riccardo, his fist banging heavily on the table-top, making all the glasses and cutlery rattle in protest. Beccy rushed from the room, and Riccardo turned his attention to Lauren.

'It's all my fault,' she began weakly. 'I knew this would happen,' she continued, shaking her head in desperation. 'I should never have married you; it was a mistake—a big mistake.'

'Mistake,' he echoed, troubled, 'to give me my daughter, to allow us all the chance to be a family?' He spoke coolly, allowing his words to penetrate.

Lauren's head shot back and she stared at him, her eyes glittering with angry contempt at his lack of understanding.

'That's typical of family life, isn't it?' she accused him. 'Angry silences because there's nothing left between us,' she mocked cruelly, 'and Beccy taking the brunt of your anger because you blame her...'

Riccardo's mouth had thinned to an angry line; his harsh features seemed as if they had been chiselled in marble. He was silent for a moment, then he said very softly, 'You know that is not true; why do you say it?'

Lauren dropped her gaze, aware of the strain he was under as he fought to control his temper. She felt confused; her heart seemed to be thudding out its own death-knell as she sat immobile, her mind racing.

'We shouldn't have got married,' she said numbly as the image of Beccy's face flashed before her, hurt and angry. 'Poor Beccy,' she murmured softly, half to herself.

'Lauren,' barked Riccardo, furious, 'Rebecca is spoilt and rude, probably because you were so desperate to make her childhood happy that you have never dared deny her anything. That's got to stop before it's too late. Secondly I suggest while Beccy's about we make every effort to show a unified front. We shall hide our true feelings for each other and give her the impression we are happy,' he concluded grimly.

Lauren looked up at him, surprised by the serious look on his face.

'Are you serious?' she asked in disbelief. 'We *pretend* to care for each other?'

'Yes; it will reassure Rebecca, and it shouldn't be too difficult as we shall be seeing less of each other soon,' he informed her crisply.

Lauren's heart sank at his words; had she driven him away? Would he just be a passing stranger at weekends?

Why should she care? she thought irritably; it would probably be best all round, she thought, waiting for his explanation.

'Well?' she snapped, unable to bear the suspense any longer. 'What's changing?' she demanded, her throat tightening as he looked at her with a cool look of amusement.

'To college,' he said simply, a smile breaking out on his face, lifting the dark storm clouds that had darkened his features.

Lauren's stomach was a whirl of butterflies as the brightness of his smile warmed her very soul.

'Aren't you a bit old for that?' she laughed, and he nodded in agreement.

'I am. You're not.'

'Me?' questioned Lauren, her heart-rate suddenly increasing and her pulse leaping at the thought. 'Me?' she repeated, unable to believe it.

'That's right; you wanted to be a teacher, didn't you?' he asked, confident of the reply. He had risen from his chair and had sauntered over to the open windows that led on to the garden and terraces.

'Yes—yes, I did,' she admitted, her mind doing somersaults as her eyes followed him. He must have remembered that had been her dearest wish all those years ago.

He turned back to face her, watching her with close intent.

'But the birth of our child prevented it,' he said, and Lauren half nodded in response, still unable to take in what he was saying. 'So before we embark on any more offspring I thought it best you fulfil your dream.'

His eyes were steadfast on her face, his body still as he watched her. Lauren could feel the million hot, sharp pins prick the backs of her eyes as she looked at him. He gave her a half-smile and stretched out his hand, and she ran instinctively towards him, wrapping her arms around his chest, hugging him till she had squeezed all the breath from his body.

'You don't know what this means to me,' she whispered as she laid her cheek on his chest and allowed him to continue holding her.

'I think I do,' he laughed, raising her head from his chest by lifting her chin.

She looked up, their eyes meeting, locking on one another. Suddenly everything seemed silent, the whole world asleep. They were transfixed, frozen in time.

It was an illusion of love, Lauren forced herself to admit later, but for now she was too lost to think of anything but how much she cared for him.

It was a bearable truce, pretending to love one another, Riccardo playing his part with remarkable skill and ease. He had spoken to Beccy about her behaviour the previous night before they had left for their picnic, and though at first she seemed a little subdued she soon returned to her normal boisterous self.

The next few days were like a dream to Lauren. It was so effortless acting as a family unit. Their days were spent sightseeing, shopping or just lazing by the pool.

Lauren gave a sigh of contentment as she rolled lazily on to her stomach, unable to move as the heat of the sun beat down on her. She abandoned her swimsuit for a much briefer bikini. It had been Riccardo's idea, and Lauren found herself wanting to agree with him more and more.

'Tired?' he asked, hearing her sigh as he sat beside her. She pushed her sunglasses from her face to look at him and smile naturally.

'No, not really,' she answered dreamily, 'just enjoying my last few days of freedom before term begins.' She frowned at the thought, and he was alerted immediately.

'You're not having second thoughts, are you?' he asked, suddenly anxious.

His question surprised her, and she wondered, Was it he who was having second thoughts?

'No, not at all; it's just that it's a bit daunting, that's all,' she said, reaching out for her suntan lotion as she felt the heat on her skin increase.

'Let me,' he offered, unfastening the clip on her top with remarkable ease—no doubt born of practice, thought Lauren with a stab of hostility. There had been

no sexual contact between them for a few days; each of
them seemed happy enough just to lie in each other's
arms, but Lauren couldn't help but wonder whether there
was another reason.

She raised herself up a little, knowing that she was
being deliberately provocative, and her top fell from her
breasts. She closed her eyes and turned her head to the
side so he could not see the smile of satisfaction that
spread across her face when she heard him give a muffled
gasp. He trickled the warm oil down her spine, and the
sensation was deliciously arousing. Then she felt his
strong hands begin to smooth the oil over her heated
shoulders. He made no attempt to touch the sides of her
breasts, which were still exposed. Instead he began a
slow, rhythmic movement down her spine, his hands
pressing lightly.

'You seem tense,' he remarked coolly, and Lauren
knew it was her own body's natural defence against him.
She remained silent, enjoying the touch of his hands on
her naked flesh. His hands had reached the base of her
spine, and a *frisson* of pleasure rippled through her body
as his fingers teased with deliberate provocation at the
rim of her bikini-bottom. He allowed his fingers to drift
with tantalising slowness across her spine, sending a
flurry of anticipation through her body, and she was
aware of the soft, slow action of his hands as he began
to descend even further.

'You can bathe in the nude; we are completely private,'
he offered, a teasing quality in his warm velvet tones.

Lauren sighed as he untied the flimsy cord that se-
cured the bikini at her sides. She swallowed nervously,
knowing full well he was aware of the effect he was
having on her. Her body began to ache as his firm hands
stroked her bare body, and she quivered with desire. But

suddenly he stopped, slapping her rear in a gesture of friendship.

'All done,' he said briefly, and Lauren suppressed her protests. Her eyes flicked over to him, but he seemed unmoved by his actions while her body was crying for fulfillment. He was stretched out on the lounger beside her, his eyes shut, and she ached to touch his body, to feel him next to her. She waited, but he remained immobile. She grinned as a solution to her problem dawned and she couldn't help but wonder if his actions were a deliberate ploy.

'Allow me,' she taunted him as she poured a pool of oil on to her palms.

Riccardo was immediately alert. His eyes shot open and he viewed her with unconcealed interest, a smoky warmth in his eyes as they drifted over her naked body. His relaxed body suddenly grew rigid as her palms were placed on his hard chest, and without even looking up she knew he was watching her. Gently she stroked his skin, enjoying the feel of it beneath her hands. She had never touched a man like this before, never had the confidence or inclination, but with Riccardo it was different.

It had always been different, she admitted to herself silently as her hands swept across his bare chest. He sucked in his breath as her hands moved further down and she toyed with the string on his brief trunks.

Lauren gave a smile of satisfaction; it was fun playing him at his own game. She poured more oil out, allowing it to trickle between his thighs, and he gave an audible gasp as she massaged the oil into his tense muscles. Licking her lips provocatively, she raised her head and smiled with slow deliberation.

'My, you are tense!' she joked, a teasing glint in her eyes. She was enjoying the sense of power his reaction was giving her. But suddenly he pulled her fiercely into his arms, and she fell against his body; feeling the hard line of his manhood pressing into her soft stomach, she gingerly moved against it, pressing herself down.

'For God's sake, Lauren, you don't know what you're doing to me,' he groaned, the rumble in his voice deep as he held her tightly. He pulled her further up till their lips met, crushing them to ease the pent-up feelings that he could barely control.

'I'm back!' yelled Beccy as she came racing through the doors, giving Lauren only seconds to grab a towel and wrap it around herself. Beccy noticed the colour on her mother's face, and stopped in surprise. She looked at her parents. 'Oops, bad timing!' she laughed cheekily, totally unperturbed by their actions.

'Beccy!' admonished Lauren in a friendly tone, but it was wasted as Beccy had already shot back inside.

Riccardo gave a groan of dismay as he realised the atmosphere had been shattered.

'I'll be glad when she starts school and I can have you all to myself,' he said, pulling Lauren back down next to him.

'Greedy,' she scolded gently, tapping his nose playfully. 'I hope she wasn't upset by us...' She paused, but Riccardo soon interrupted.

'No, it is natural in a loving relationship; she understands that already, while you are still learning,' he whispered in her ear, the warmth of his breath making her attentive. Lauren drew away reluctantly and stood up.

'Let's go out to dinner,' she said, suddenly feeling the desire to celebrate.

'As a family?' he asked.

'Of course.'

'OK,' he agreed reluctantly. 'But I'll have you alone sooner or later,' he warned with a deliciously wicked grin on his face. Lauren acknowledged it with one of her own.

'Is that a threat or a promise?' she teased playfully, enjoying the banter between them.

'Both!' he replied emphatically as he watched her walk away, enjoying the supple movements of her body.

The night was perfect, the sky burnished with the red-hot glow of an evening sun sinking peacefully behind the backdrop of Florence, its red rays tinting the already red roofs with a fiery glint. The sweet smell of lemons hung in the air and a cool breeze carried the singing of the crickets throughout the villa. Lauren sighed with a contentment and peace she had never thought possible. She felt at home at last.

She turned as she heard Riccardo's and Beccy's voices.

'Here you are!' Riccardo exclaimed, looking at her with desire and a smile that seared her soul. 'Are you ready? We are going somewhere rather special,' he said, holding out his hand to her. Lauren took it with a naturalness that made his heart soar, and he clasped her hand tightly in his.

La Torre was an excellent restaurant situated in the Piazza Umberto, and the food was wonderful. Both Riccardo and Lauren ate the *stracotto di vitellone*—thick chunks of veal stewed in the local Chianti wine. Beccy was happy just with a pasta dish, but she couldn't resist the selection of desserts. It was so good to be sitting just like a family, eating together and sharing the day's events.

'Am I going to be a sister soon?' Beccy suddenly announced, unaware of the embarrassment she caused Lauren, who flushed immediately.

Riccardo raised his eyebrows to heaven in mock horror.

'I think one of you is bad enough,' he teased her, and she laughed good-naturedly as Riccardo turned his attention to Lauren, his eyes questioning.

'I thought the idea was I was going to qualify as a teacher,' she reminded him, sipping her wine and allowing her eyes to peep over the rim of her glass.

'Couldn't you do both?' he asked; there was almost a plea in his voice.

Lauren smiled as she lowered her glass. 'I could manage to qualify without your help, but I certainly need your help in the other department,' she laughed, waiting for his reaction.

'You've got it,' he answered quite seriously, taking her hand to his mouth and kissing it gently, the hot touch of his lips sending a ripple of pleasure through her body. The feeling that passed between them was electric; suddenly Lauren felt more alive than she had ever done in her life.

The rest of the evening was perfect, but both parents were glad to see Beccy safely in bed.

'Fancy a nightcap?' offered Riccardo, pulling at his tie and unbuttoning his top shirt button.

Lauren nodded as she followed him downstairs.

'Let's go outside—it's still warm,' she called as he went to fix the drinks. She heard the pop of the champagne cork and turned. 'What are we celebrating?' she asked, taking the glass and sipping the ice-cold liquid. It was delicious, fragrant and lively.

'Us,' he answered simply as he poured himself another glass.

They sat together on a swinging bench, Lauren leaning gently on his shoulder, enjoying the intimacy between them. There was no need for words any longer; she felt totally at peace, and knew Riccardo did too.

'Lauren?' he asked, his voice shattering the stillness of the night. 'You're happy here, aren't you?'

'Yes,' she answered immediately, wondering what had prompted such a question. The night was too dark for her to see the doubt in his eyes.

'I want us to be happy—a real happy family,' he added softly, drawing her close, and for once Lauren did not find the thought frightening.

'So do I,' she murmured, trying to dispel the last few niggling doubts she had. She snuggled up closer to him, and he found it impossible to ignore the soft feel of her curvaceous body moulding into his.

He groaned as he lowered his head to kiss her. Lauren was aware of the effect she was having on him, and gave a relaxed sigh of pleasure as his firm lips touched her yielding mouth. She had longed for this moment all day, her body aching for his touch. Her pulse leapt and her world began to spin crazily as his mouth captured hers. She was aware of nothing but the sensation of his body next to hers and the crushing demand of his lips, and responded with equal desire, drawing him closer to her as his tongue teased her open mouth. She shuddered with delight, and he took her gently by the hand and led her upstairs.

She looked at him as he closed the bedroom door softly behind them. His eyes were like pools of melted chocolate, deep, warm and inviting. For a few minutes neither of them moved, then he wrapped his arms around her, lifted her into his arms with ease and carried her to the bed. He lifted the thin, silky top she was wearing and she helped him draw it over her head and toss it carelessly to one side.

He gasped at the beauty of her breasts, swelling with anticipation in their lacy top. He smoothed his hands over them, and she gave a moan as her body went into spasm. He kissed her lightly on the lips then moved to her neck and descended, kissing the valley between her breasts. Soon his lips moved lower, kissing the flatness of her stomach till she quivered in delight. His hands reached the waistband of her skirt and he unfastened it deftly as she raised her hips to allow him to slide it off.

His lips continued the downward path, Lauren stiffening, her stomach in violent contraction as he kissed her inner thighs. He stopped and looked up at her, and she smiled dreamily as she watched him undress. His clothes were soon discarded in an untidy heap on the floor. She liked looking at his body—it fired her arousal. His body was lean and hard, his muscles clearly defined without being obvious.

She took a calming breath as he lay next to her. For a moment neither of them moved, but allowed themselves to appreciate each other's bodies, and then slowly, gently they moved together. Her hair was laid out over the pillows like a great golden cloud and her usually pale eyes were darkened and misty with passion. She looked up at him, he face bereft of any doubts, her mind clear, and she arched her body to meet him. The knowledge that she was at last so trusting held him in wonder, and he lowered his head to kiss her tender, eager mouth. Lauren stroked his back, her hands gliding around the front of his chest, and she rubbed the firm mat of dark hairs, enjoying the sensation of it between her fingers.

He tossed aside her lacy underwear and stroked her body, welcoming the deep feeling of love he felt as she willingly welcomed his strength. She arched her hips and he held her as he moved against her till they finally became one in a union of loving spirit and body. He moved with slow, rhythmic care, and she moaned as his speed naturally increased till they were thrusting against each other, unable to stop. She clung desperately to him as the first wave of passion swept over her and she gave a cry as her mind floated away into oblivion, the crescendo of fervour continuing to mount till their bodies shook in convulsive union. Lauren called his name as she felt her body soar, and he held her tightly, not wanting to break the intimacy they had known.

The quiet stillness that followed was only interrupted by their heavy, deep breaths. They lay locked together, clinging to each other like shipwrecks on a sea of desire, unwilling to be parted. Finally he moved away, but kept his arm tightly around her, taking her with him. They lay side by side, Lauren curled up in the crook of his arm, her body damp with perspiration. He looked down at her and the dreamy look that met his eyes made him smile.

Lauren closed her eyes, content not to speak for fear it would shatter the beauty of what had passed between them. This truly was different—tonight they had made love. She smiled and freely acknowledged it was true: she loved Riccardo and he loved her.

CHAPTER TEN

IT WAS as if someone had washed the world for Lauren. The sky appeared bluer, the sun so much brighter, the air suddenly so much fresher. The grass and the trees were dressed in vivid green and the flowers bloomed with such a fine array of colours. She felt young again and alive, so alive that there was a briskness in her step and a ready smile on her soft lips. She hummed to herself constantly, often breaking into song when she was unable to contain her happiness any longer.

It was perfect. At last, after all these years of pain and self-doubt, she was finally happy; being in love and being loved was the most marvellous thing in the world. She had begun college, and though she had found it difficult nothing could suppress her enthusiasm.

Riccardo watched Lauren as she flowered; she reminded him of a small rosebud opening up before him; each day another beautiful petal was revealed. Every evening he waited patiently for her return, longing to hear her news, anxious if she was only moments late. Today he frowned as he looked at the clock; she was certainly late this evening, he thought. He caught Beccy watching him, and smiled.

'She will be here shortly,' he said, wondering whom he was trying to reassure. He wanted to trust her, to allow her as much freedom as she wanted, but it was difficult when he was so afraid of losing her again. However, the sound of her voice in the hall dispelled the niggling doubts which pervaded his mind, and he scolded himself inwardly for doubting her at all.

'*Ciao*,' smiled Lauren, kissing him lightly on the cheek; she sensed something was wrong. She was sensitive to his mood and was troubled by it. 'Is there something the matter?' she asked, searching his face for an answer.

He smiled, pleased by her concern. 'No, you were a little late, that's all.'

'Yes, the lecture ran a little over time,' she admitted, flopping into a chair and kicking her shoes off. She began to massage her toes, unaware of the darkening of his eyes as he studied her. She looked different; there was something in her face—she was carrying a hidden secret.

'I think I'll take a shower before dinner,' she said, resting back and closing her eyes. It was hard work going back to studying after all this time, and the strain was beginning to tell.

'Yes, go and have a shower—Tonio and Marcella are coming over later,' he said casually, watching her with intent. He was looking forward to an evening with friends; they would help him forget the devils that tormented him.

Lauren groaned. 'Oh, I'm sorry, Riccardo, but I forgot all about that, and I've an essay to finish by tomorrow,' she explained, rubbing her forehead as she struggled to think of a solution.

'Forget your essay—they're my friends, our guests,' he snapped, his eyes flashing at her.

'I can't; you know how much this means to me...' she began, but the building storm of anger that swirled in his eyes silenced her. She sighed. 'I'll do it after they're gone,' she said wearily as she dragged herself upstairs.

She flung her clothes on to the floor in the bedroom, her mind racing. It was proving far harder than she imagined it would be. She stood under the shower, allowing the hot water that pumped forcefully over her to wash away the tiredness of the day. She shampooed her hair—it had been looking dull recently, and she constantly felt tired.

She gave a loud sigh as she pulled her hair from her face and looked at her reflection critically. The warm sun had coloured her usually pale face, giving her complexion a special glow, and she smiled at herself as her hand drifted to her stomach. Maybe tiredness was due to something else, she mused, her smile widening at the thought. It was too early to say, and she wanted to be certain before she said anything. She resolved to make an immediate appointment at the doctor's.

She slipped her robe on and went to the phone; it took an age to find the number, and just as it was finally answered Riccardo came into the room. Lauren panicked, immediately crashing the phone back on to its cradle and jumping to her feet.

'Who are you ringing?' Riccardo demanded as the telephone book fell to the floor with a dull thud. Lauren felt a stinging red colour flood her face and she lowered her eyes to avoid his steely glare. His eyes narrowed on hers; she had no friends as yet—who would she be calling? All his doubts resurfaced with a vengeance.

'A—a fellow student,' she stammered, knowing herself that she didn't sound that sure.

Riccardo raised the dark wing of his eyebrow and viewed her with a coolness that froze her heart. There was something dark and unreadable in his eyes, and she felt herself colour still further. She longed to tell him, but it would spoil the surprise—in twenty-four hours she could tell him the truth.

'I needed to check a couple of facts,' she continued, her voice shaky as the atmosphere in the room seemed to chill and he continued to stare at her, his face as rigid as stone.

'Really,' he drawled, his stomach tightening as he spoke. 'And did you get the information you wanted?' he asked drily.

Lauren felt her face suffuse with colour again, her heart-rate increase. She hated this deceit, and she lowered her eyes to prevent him from seeing her lies.

'Yes, yes, I did, thanks,' she said shakily as she made her way over to her dressing-table.

Riccardo caught her wrist as she passed, and Lauren's head snapped back in amazement to look at him. His face was dark and forbidding, and she gave a shiver. She stood totally rigid, her heart thudding painfully inside her chest just watching him and seeing the detail of his face.

When he spoke, his voice was as steely as the look in his eyes.

'Lauren...' he began, but suddenly broke off, dropping her hand as he turned away. 'Never mind,' he said.

'No, wait.' She forced herself to follow him; she couldn't bear the look in his eyes. 'What were you going to say?' she asked, watching him intently.

He shrugged his powerful shoulders and his dark eyes flicked over her, his face harsh.

'It doesn't matter,' he said in a clipped tone. He gave her a tight smile. 'Look your best tonight,' he added as he closed the door behind him.

Lauren stood staring at the closed door, the enveloping silence chilling her heart. She closed her eyes to shut out the painful memory of his grim face. He doesn't really trust me, she thought bitterly. She could read the distrust in his eyes but consoled herself with the thought of the wonderful secret she was guarding so carefully.

It was time for dinner before Lauren left her room. The meal was filled with Beccy's endless chatter, and Lauren's fears subsided when she heard Riccardo asking

Beccy about her day with unfeigned interest. Simonetta took Beccy away after dinner, and Lauren and Riccardo sat awaiting their guests. Riccardo was strangely silent, and Lauren busied herself making notes with a furious hand as the deadline for her essay drew closer.

Finally she heard the sound of a car drawing up outside, and hastily put away her papers. She liked Marcella a lot. She was an American and had been living in Florence for the past six years. Tonio and she had fallen madly in love in a whirlwind affair, and they had married within two months of meeting. They had now been happily married for five years, and had a two-year-old son called Joel. Lauren kissed them both warmly and escorted them inside. Tonio immediately started talking business with Riccardo, and the two women decided to take their drinks outside. Once seated, Marcella began to question Lauren.

'Hey, have you two had a fight?' she laughed, but the concern in her voice was evident, and she gave a frown as she spoke.

Lauren's head shot up, a look of distress on her face.

'No, not at all,' she denied immediately.

'Aw, come on, honey,' persuaded Marcella, leaning over and resting her hand on Lauren's.

Lauren could feel hot pin-pricks at the backs of her eyes, but she didn't know why. They hadn't really argued.

'No, it's not that...' She paused before suddenly blurting out in a whisper, 'I think I may be pregnant,' moving closer to Marcella, unaware of the studying look Riccardo was giving her.

'Congratulations...but Riccardo doesn't want a child?' suggested Marcella.

'Oh, yes, of course he does—well, he will once I tell him,' Lauren said, glad to have someone to talk to.

'Then tell him, for God's sake.'

'I can't—not yet; I haven't had it confirmed. I thought I'd find a doctor first——' Lauren began to explain, but Marcella immediately interrupted.

'No problem, use mine; he was fantastic and totally bilingual, so you'll have no problems,' she enthused warmly.

Lauren flushed with pleasure. 'That's very kind of you...'

'Hey, we just want to be the godparents—deal?' laughed Marcella, and Lauren smiled back.

The women talked in conspiratorial whispers about pregnancy, frightened they would be overheard. Lauren sometimes felt she was being watched, and often when she looked up she would see Riccardo's dark eyes fastened upon her, dark, deep and unreadable. She smiled at him, but he seemed oblivious to her, as if he was staring right through her. Lauren tried to dismiss the idea as fanciful, but there was a niggling doubt in her mind, and she was grateful when Tonio and Marcella finally left. She closed the door and sighed; she felt drained, and leant against the door.

'Let's go to bed,' whispered Riccardo, wrapping his arm around her waist.

Lauren stiffened and moved away; she knew her weakness when he was around, and was still determined to finish the essay.

'No, you go up—I've this essay to write,' she told him firmly, a coolness in her voice as she moved away. Riccardo frowned deeply and walked upstairs, casting a puzzled look down on his wife as she buried her head in a pile of papers.

Lauren was engrossed when the phone suddenly rang, its shrill tone piercing the silent night air. She darted up at once to answer it.

'Marcella!' she whispered, not wishing to disturb Riccardo. 'What on earth . . . ?' she asked.

'Here's my doctor's number—give him a ring first thing tomorrow; he's bound to fit you in.'

'Tomorrow? That's a bit short notice——' began Lauren after she had taken down the number, but Marcella had already gone, and as she could hear Joel crying she replaced the receiver and folded the quickly written number in her hand.

She jumped as she turned and faced Riccardo, and moistened her suddenly dry lips, eyeing him warily, wondering how much he had heard. Her whole body was tense and an icy chill ran down her spine. Riccardo smiled, and she saw his glistening teeth flash.

'Who was that?' he asked, his voice dangerously soft and quiet. Lauren swallowed, her throat parched.

'Marcella,' she answered, hoping he wouldn't question further.

'Really?' he drawled, his voice chilling. 'Now what could she possibly want? You have talked all evening,' he queried, a frown furrowing his brow and his jaw clenching.

'Women's talk, nothing else,' answered Lauren in an attempt to keep her voice calm and dispel any suspicions.

He nodded briefly, his eyes glittering with flashes of light.

'Don't stay up too late,' he warned, looking at the stray piece of paper that protruded from her hand. He went back up the stairs silently, his back stiff, deep in thought. Lauren breathed a sigh of relief; she couldn't wait for tomorrow, and held the telephone number safely in her tight fist.

It was several hours later before she was satisfied with her paper. She closed her books and ran a weary hand across her face. She was shattered, and a few minutes later she slid silently into bed. Riccardo was already in a deep sleep.

A gentle kiss on her face awoke her; she couldn't believe it was morning so soon. Riccardo moved closer, the warm strength of his body next to hers, and pulled her towards him, a hunger in his eyes.

'I waited for you, but I must have fallen asleep,' he said apologetically as his masterful hands stroked her body.

Lauren gave a weak smile; a feeling of nausea began to come over her. She jumped from the bed, hurrying for the bathroom, where she leant against the cool tiled walls as a prickly heat covered her and her stomach swayed uncontrollably. Riccardo lay in bed, a cold, furious anger building inside him; never before had his touch been so abhorrent to her.

Lauren soon recovered; she took a shower, and felt a little better. She dressed with care, wanting to look her best when she visited the doctor.

'Going anywhere special today?' asked Riccardo tightly, watching her, his eyes narrowing. He could see she had made an effort with her appearance, and it troubled him.

'No, I've to give in my essay and attend one lecture, that's all,' she answered in half-truths, aware of the twin flags of colour that had risen on her face.

He nodded briefly, his face rigid, and straightened his tie, having dressed while she showered.

'See you tonight, then,' he said as he planted a cool kiss on her cheek and left for his office.

Lauren snatched up the phone the moment he was gone. She was delighted that if she went this morning the result of her test would be available by late afternoon, and left home immediately, calling a hurried goodbye to Beccy.

The lecture finished by eleven-thirty, but Lauren was far too excited to go home; she decided to stay in town and pick up her results from the doctor then go home. Florence was a delight as usual, and Lauren knew so many of the students that there were calls greeting her from every side.

'Lauren, Lauren!' The voice was so distinctly English that she turned round.

'Mitchell!' She gave a cry of pleasure as she saw his familiar boyish face grinning at her. 'What on earth are you doing here?' she asked in total amazement.

'I'm on holiday,' he laughed, but he added seriously, 'I chose Florence for a reason. I hoped I'd bump into you, to see how you were getting on.'

Lauren kissed him lightly on the cheek.

'I love you—you're so kind. Let's go and eat, and I'll tell you all about it.'

They linked hands and walked down one of the narrow streets to find a cheap place for lunch. Lauren had not noticed the sharp eyes of Maria or sensed her presence as she followed them silently down the cobbled road. They sat together, Lauren bursting to tell Mitchell that all was fine. They ordered a simple pasta dish with a fresh green salad and garlic bread, and Lauren was snapping a bread stick when she saw Maria half in, half out of a shop doorway. She called immediately.

'Maria, come and join us for lunch.'

Maria looked strange for a moment before reluctantly joining them.

'I will not stop—I've got things to do,' she explained, looking at Mitchell and awaiting an introduction.

'Maria, Mitchell. Mitchell, Maria,' supplied Lauren as the pair of them shook hands cordially.

'I'd love to stay, but I've a pressing engagement,' Maria said hurriedly before darting away.

Lauren shrugged and turned her attention back on Mitchell. She could sense his disappointment when she explained how happy she was and gave him the news that perhaps she was already with child. But he smiled bravely, gave her his best wishes, and Lauren was glad to have seen him again. She had now rid herself of any memories of the past. She now felt she could face the future confident in her loving marriage.

The best part of her day, though, was when her pregnancy was confirmed; she had not thought it possible so soon. Then she smiled; they had hardly been celibate since the wedding, she admitted to herself ruefully.

She was so happy that she practically ran home; she ached to tell Riccardo the news, it was so exciting, and this time it would be so different.

She arranged for Simonetta and Beccy to go out for the evening, visit some schoolfriends, and for a special dinner to be prepared, champagne to be left chilling. She wanted everything to be just perfect—a complete contrast to last time. The joy she felt was bubbling up inside her and the hours seemed to drag. She bathed with care, filling the bath with scents and oils and splashing the water over her flat stomach in a slow, caressing rhythm. She was already thinking of names, of where to place the nursery, and she smiled a secret smile.

She spent an age getting ready, applying make-up with care, brushing her hair till it fell about her shoulders in a billowing golden halo.

At last she was ready; she heard Riccardo's voice in the hall. She had wanted to wait to tell him over dinner, but the moment she heard his voice she knew she could wait no longer. She rushed to the door, but paused at the top of the stairs and peeped over the hand-rail. She did not recognise the other voice, which was definitely female and English.

Lauren watched the scene in horror, as Riccardo kissed the woman and said, 'The same arrangement as usual, but remember—I'm married now, so only while she is not here,' he explained, and the squeal of laughter from the woman made her heart sink even further.

'Of course—I understand,' she laughed. 'Till to-morrow, then,' she called as she left.

Lauren stood transfixed, locked into immobility as the awful realisation struck her. She ran back into her bathroom, leaning over the basin as the waves of sickness washed over her. Hot tears sprang to her eyes and fell silently down her face. She felt wretched.

Her mind automatically went back to the last time she was faced with this scenario. It was all the same. Once she had become a conquest in his arms, willingly giving herself to him in love, he had lost interest. The bitterness that swelled up made her throat feel harsh and painful. He was unfaithful while promising her a happy family life.

A deep frown furrowed Lauren's forehead as she tried to think; was she to blame? Had she destroyed this family as she had destroyed others? She sank despairingly on to the bathroom stool, her head whirling. She was pregnant again to a man who cared nothing for her. The true enormity of the situation she was facing was hard to reckon with.

She heard Riccardo call and stiffened immediately; how was she to react? She looked at herself in the mirror and did a quick repair on her make-up. She at least would have her pride if nothing else. She would face him with his adultery and she would demand a divorce.

Lauren sighed miserably; she had known all along that this would happen, but now she had complicated things even further. She loved Riccardo, loved the unborn child she was carrying. 'God, what a mess!' she mumbled to herself, bracing her shoulders and descending the stairs with as much dignity as she possessed.

Riccardo was standing looking out of the window, and he turned as she entered, his eyebrows rising as he saw her.

He wore a grim expression, and Lauren wondered if he realised he had been overheard.

'You're looking lovely this evening.' There was a note of mockery in his teasing voice, and she caught the smell of alcohol, and knew at once he had been drinking—possibly too much. Her heart thumped violently as she stared at him, feeling her knees weaken, and rendered totally speechless by the glacial look in his eyes.

'Who are you all dressed up for, Lauren?' he asked, his mouth tight and angry. His face was dark and his cheek jerking as he controlled his temper. There was something wrong; she could sense it. Maybe Marcella had told him about the child, and as he wasn't really in love with her perhaps he saw it as a burden. She managed to swallow, and stepped nearer to him but he drew away from her, a flash of fury darkening his face.

'Where have you been today?' he asked coolly, his sharp eyes fixed on hers.

'You know where I've been; why do you ask?' she countered; the atmosphere was tense but she was determined to remain calm, to present an unconcerned façade. She knew he was going to tell her it was over; she could sense the pent-up anger and frustration.

'I know what you tell me,' he countered grimly, turning away from her, his back stiff and unforgiving.

'I tell you the truth,' she snapped back, his betrayal of her filling her mind. He swung round, his jaw firm and his eyes flashing with glints of anger.

'Truth!' he scoffed, a cruel smile of derision on his face. 'I'm going away. Business,' he snapped. 'No doubt you can keep yourself occupied while I'm away,' he sneered.

'We have to talk, Riccardo,' she began as she sank into a chair, amazed at the composure in her voice.

He looked at her contemptuously, and her heart shrivelled up within her. He gave a hollow laugh.

'Yes,' he agreed, his tone frosty. 'We shall talk when I return.' There was a grim finality in his tone that Lauren understood.

'I s-see,' she managed to stutter bravely, not allowing the tears to fall.

He left her alone, and moments later she heard the harsh slam of the door and the roar of his car engine as he drove away. It was then that Lauren allowed herself to cry. All the plans she had made, all the dreams had been shattered, torn apart, and once again she was left with nothing.

The next three days seemed to last an eternity. Lauren waited, hoping each time the phone rang that it would be Riccardo, but he made no attempt to get in touch. She tried to put on a brave face, continuing her studies, and she was grateful that Beccy had settled down so well, that she had her own friends. She was so well occupied that she seemed unaware that Riccardo was not around, but Lauren finally decided she should broach the subject to allow Beccy some time to come to terms with what was happening.

'Beccy,' she began over dinner on the third evening, 'Riccardo is away, working somewhere, and I'm not sure——' Lauren said no more because Beccy immediately interrupted.

'No, he's not; when he phoned the other day——' she informed her mother, but she was stopped in mid-sentence as a spiral of fear raced down Lauren's spine and she interjected in a high voice, her anxiety obvious,

'You spoke to him? What did he say? What did he want? Where is he?' The torrent of questions spilled from Lauren; she might have known he would want to keep Beccy, and the thought made her panic.

Beccy looked stunned as her mother jumped from her chair and clasped her arm tightly.

'Did he want you to meet him somewhere?' she questioned her, her eyes wide with fear and the pounding of her heart thudding through her brain.

Beccy shook her head. 'No!' she cried emphatically, shaking herself free from her mother's arms. 'He just wanted to know how we all were. I asked him when he was coming home, and he said he didn't know,' she informed her mother in a bored tone.

'You know where he is, though?' Lauren asked, swallowing the lump of fear that was rising in her throat.

'Yeah,' drawled Beccy, 'he's at that house he had built, near the church.'

'Monastery,' corrected Lauren without thinking, her mind racing. 'I'm going to see him tomorrow; it's about time I saw this house,' she mused, half to herself.

'Can I come?' pleaded Beccy, already sensing a refusal.

'No. I want to see him alone,' Lauren said coolly, unaware that her eyes had softened with the tears that pricked behind them.

The rest of the evening was spent watching television, and Lauren was grateful when it was time for bed. She wanted the morning to come as quickly as possible; she wanted to face him, to sort everything out. She couldn't live with the threat of him taking Beccy. She had been foolish enough to fall in love with him all over again, and with bitter irony history seemed determined to repeat itself.

The next morning Lauren took the road to Pratolino, but she was immune to the beautiful scenery; all her thoughts were on Riccardo. She drove carefully, ignoring the irate Italian drivers who sounded their horns relentlessly at her as she refused to increase her speed to their death-defying rate.

Finally Lauren gasped as the road straightened after a bend, and there before her was the tiny little cottage she had shared so often with Riccardo. The cottage was untouched; the same windows, door, the multitude of window-boxes and hanging baskets still adorning the exterior. It looked even more beautiful, freshly painted with a new red pantile roof.

She stopped the car outside the door, forcing herself to forget all the happiness she had known there, and looked cautiously through the window; but Riccardo was not in sight. She tugged at the rope and heard the shrill ring of the bell in the distance. Her heart was fluttering like a trapped butterfly, and she suddenly thought he might not be alone. She swallowed nervously, trying to dismiss the thought, but it haunted her mind till the pain was almost unbearable.

Suddenly the door opened with a flourish, and the surprise on Riccardo's face convinced Lauren he was not alone. For a moment neither of them spoke, but just stood staring at each other with cold, angry eyes.

'Come in,' he snapped, stepping back to allow her to enter, but there was no welcome in his voice and his politeness was a thin veneer. Lauren mumbled her thanks as she passed him, and stepped into what used to be the tiny lounge; now it was a huge square hall, and she gave a cry of surprise—it was in complete contrast to the outside of the building, and for a moment she remembered how she had often toyed with the idea that it would make a marvellous family home. She had scribbled down ideas, and Riccardo had laughed at her ambitions.

As if reading her mind, he broke into her thoughts.

'You still think it would make an ideal family home?' The crispness of his tone warned her that he was not pleased by her arrival, and she swung round, ready to face him. She was not going to run this time, nor was she going to live in fear for her children's safety.

'It's beautiful, and in other circumstances I would enjoy seeing the rest of it; however, there are more important things to discuss.' The composure in her voice surprised her, and she faced him with a calmness she had not believed possible.

'You want a divorce,' he spat at her bitterly, staring fixedly at her, his eyes flashing.

Lauren felt herself shiver, and she wrung her hands as she nodded, tears stinging her eyes. She wondered how he knew; perhaps he had deliberately allowed her to see him with the English woman.

'Why, Lauren? Did I not make you happy?' he asked. There was an angry plea in his voice, and for a moment her heart went out to him. But she had her self-respect; she couldn't be party to a marriage based on such a relationship. She wanted his love totally. She would not share him.

'It's over, Riccardo; I thought you'd changed, but you haven't...' She mumbled the words, which hurt her more than he knew.

His lips twisted bitterly, his eyes burning with raw emotion.

'No more than you have,' he snapped back through clenched teeth, and Lauren could see the fury building in his eyes. She glared at him, knowing she loved him even while he cheated on her. What right did he have for anger? She was too choked to speak, her emotions running too high. The chasm between them was widening all the time.

'What do you mean by that?' she asked, suddenly angry at his subtle innuendoes. He was breathing harshly as he grabbed her wrist, the pain and anger etched deep into his chiselled features.

'You ask me that?' he said scornfully, his eyes glittering with temper. 'You're the guilty party,' he sneered, the thin veneer of control he had had wearing thin.

Lauren pulled away, rubbing at the tender spots around her wrists.

'The only thing I'm guilty of, Riccardo, is being foolish enough to think I loved you.'

'Love!' he scoffed, turning from her. 'What do you know of love? The pain of wanting someone, of thinking at last they are yours only to find out——'

He stopped and turned on her, his eyes shining with a cold brilliance that frightened her. She gasped as she saw the anger cut deep into his face. 'You have a lover,' he spat at her, the contempt evident in his voice.

Lauren stared at him in disbelief, unable to understand such an accusation.

'How dare you accuse me to ease your own conscience?' she flung back at him loathingly.

'You think I'm having an affair?' he ground out between clenched teeth.

There was a silence as she looked at him, amazed at his composure.

'I know you are. I thought perhaps you had grown out of your need to seduce every female that came your way,' she said miserably as her head sank in defeat.

'What are you talking about?' he growled, pulling her down on to the couch and facing her, his expression grim and fearful.

Lauren swallowed the rising lump of panic, but it was too late to go back now; she had faced up to reality, so could he.

'Ten years ago you amused yourself seducing virgins— I was one of them. Only I had to pay a higher price than most. I thought you loved me, would want my child. I was wrong. It seems I still am,' she confessed simply as her heart shattered into a thousand pieces, the shards hitting every nerve in her body.

He sat up, pulling her roughly into his arms till her face was only inches away from his. He was shaking her as he roared, 'What on earth makes you think that? It's just plain stupid.'

'I saw you the other night; I was willing to forget the past, put it behind us...' she faltered as tears sprang to her eyes. 'I heard you make arrangements with her, telling her to make sure I wasn't around,' she told him, lifting her face to look at his and enjoying his stunned expression.

'Clare? You mean Clare?' he asked, his voice surprisingly calm; but he still held her arms in a tight grip.

Lauren nodded numbly, and Riccardo sighed and shook his head.

'Clare is our neighbour during the summer months. I allow her to use our pool. She is very happily married, has six children, and only last month became a grandmother. You see how you jump to conclusions, judging me by your own miserable standards?' he said thickly, his grip tightening.

Lauren stared, unable to speak as she realised he was telling the truth.

'I—I'm sorry,' she faltered uneasily. 'I thought...'

'But you, Lauren, you have cheated me—twice!' he said threateningly. 'First you rob me of my daughter, then you take up with your lover only months after our marriage,' he said, his voice full of disdain.

Lauren shot to her feet, shaken by his accusation, disgusted and alarmed by it.

'I haven't got a lover—what gave you that idea?' she demanded hoarsely.

'Your innocence does you credit,' he mocked, his eyes narrowing to diamond chips as he viewed her. 'You think I am stupid; did I not suspect when you came home from college late? Then you whisper all evening with Marcella—the discreet telephone call, the note you hid from me.'

Lauren listened in amazement; she could see how it would look, but if he truly loved her, truly trusted her...

'Because of this you accuse me of having an affair?' she retorted. 'Have you no trust, no faith in me? Do you have any love for me at all?' She tried to keep the plea from her voice, but failed.

'Oh, Lauren, you dress the other morning with such care yet you tell me it is just for one lecture. You do not come home till late afternoon, but you forget you told me you had only one lecture,' he repeated, disgusted by her actions. 'My accusation is sound; you were seen— you and Mitchell meeting, kissing, having lunch together.'

There was a sadness in his voice she had not expected to hear, and for a moment she saw a glimmer of hope. Someone had been deliberately making mischief between them, hoping that their marriage would fail.

'Maria,' she said coldly, slowly, piecing together the jigsaw.

Riccardo nodded. 'Yes, it was Maria who told me the truth,' he agreed.

'Maria also told me all those years ago that I was one young English girl among many. It was she who gave me the money to return to England—remember, Riccardo? She was here the night I came to tell you the news of my pregnancy, who put the doubt in your mind that the child might be someone else's.'

Riccardo's eyes turned as black as the night, his jaw suddenly tensed, and a nerve throbbed repeatedly at his throat. Lauren relaxed, knowing that now he accepted what she was saying.

'The bitch!' he spat out, leaping to his feet, his temper about to erupt. 'But why should she do such a thing?' he demanded.

Lauren looked up at him and shook her head.

'Because she loves you. Wants you.'

'Maria?' he echoed in disbelief. 'We are like brother and sister. Our families are as one; why would she think such foolishness?'

'We believe all manner of things when we love someone,' said Lauren wisely, thinking how easily they had both accepted Maria's lies.

He said nothing, and they both remained silent as they thought over what had passed between them. It had all been a misunderstanding. He sank back down on the couch beside her, his eyes suddenly tender, soft.

'I want to believe you, Lauren...' He paused.

'I lied; Mitchell has never been my lover. There has only ever been you, but I was so angry, I said that to hurt you. Forgive me?' she asked.

'Will you forgive me for doubting you for all those wasted years?' he asked.

She nodded as she snuggled closer to him.

'Lauren,' he asked again, 'why all the secrecy? I thought when I came home and Beccy had gone that you had made arrangements to leave with Mitchell. If that's not true, what's going on?' he asked, puzzled.

Lauren gave a slow, secret smile.

'The whispers between me and Marcella, the secret telephone call and number, the reason I was late back from college, and the reason I came here today is...' She was enjoying the suspense, the look of anxiety on his face. 'I've been to the doctor,' she finished.

Riccardo paled and his expression changed to one of alarm.

'If you're ill I'll have the best doctors here by tomorrow,' he assured her.

She couldn't bear to tease him any longer; she began to laugh and shook her head.

'I'm not ill, I'm pregnant,' she explained.

Riccardo stared at her, his eyes growing soft with unshed tears as he held her close. Tentatively he drew his hand gently across her stomach and patted the new life that was already stirring below.

'Our child,' he said wistfully.

Lauren moved even closer to him and gave a happy sigh. 'We are a happy family at last,' she murmured.

'Here, Lauren, here we shall raise our family. In this house, which I had built as a panacea to forget you—now at last it shall be lived in,' he said, drawing her even closer to him.

She no longer needed to hear him say the words 'I love you'; every action, every deed, every word he spoke was confirmation of that fact. He lowered his head to hers; she watched him drawing closer till his features became a blur and she allowed him to capture her soft eager lips. His arms slid around her tightly, his hot mouth taking hers while he crushed her against him. His mouth moved with renewed urgency, and a mutual fire seemed to ignite them both. She clung to him as her body turned to liquid, and she could feel his burning desire.

Riccardo raised his head, his breath ragged, and he whispered hoarsely, 'I love you, Lauren; I've always loved you.'

Lauren buried her head deep in his chest to prevent him from seeing the hot tears that flowed. She had thought no one would ever say those words to her, and the effect was overwhelming.

'What's the matter?' he asked gently, raising her head by lifting her chin.

'You've never said that before,' she muttered, a tremble in her voice.

'Then you had better get used to it, because I'll be saying it a lot. I love you, I love you, I love——'

But Lauren could stand it no longer. She grasped his neck and drew him down, kissing him fiercely.

SPRING IS IN THE AIR . . .

AND SO IS ROMANCE

Springtime Romance – A collection of stories
from four popular Mills & Boon authors, which
we know you will enjoy this Springtime.

GENTLE SAVAGE   –   Helen Brooks
SNOWDROPS FOR A BRIDE   –   Grace Green
POSEIDON'S DAUGHTER   –   Jessica Hart
EXTREME PROVOCATION   –   Sarah Holland

Available April 1993   Price £6.80

Accept 4 FREE Romances and 2 FREE gifts

Mills & Boon

FROM READER SERVICE

An irresistible invitation from Mills & Boon Reader Service. Please accept our offer of 4 free Romances, a CUDDLY TEDDY and a special MYSTERY GIFT... Then, if you choose, go on to enjoy 6 captivating Romances every month for just £1.70 each, postage and packing free. Plus our FREE Newsletter with author news, competitions and much more.

**Send the coupon below to:
Reader Service, FREEPOST,
PO Box 236, Croydon,
Surrey CR9 9EL.**

NO STAMP REQUIRED

Yes! Please rush me 4 Free Romances and 2 free gifts!

Please also reserve me a Reader Service Subscription. If I decide to subscribe I can look forward to receiving 6 brand new Romances each month for just £10.20, post and packing free.

If I choose not to subscribe I shall write to you within 10 days - I can keep the books and gifts whatever I decide. I may cancel or suspend my subscription at any time. I am over 18 years of age.

Ms/Mrs/Miss/Mr ———————————————————————— EP30R

Address ————————————————————————

————————————————————————

Postcode ——————————— Signature ———————————

Next Month's Romances

Each month you can choose from a wide variety of romance with Mills & Boon. Below are the new titles to look out for next month, why not ask either Mills & Boon Reader Service or your Newsagent to reserve you a copy of the titles you want to buy — just tick the titles you would like and either post to Reader Service or take it to any Newsagent and ask them to order your books.

Please save me the following titles:	Please tick	√
BABY MAKES THREE	Emma Goldrick	
BETH AND THE BARBARIAN	Miranda Lee	
GRACIOUS LADY	Carole Mortimer	
THE HAWK AND THE LAMB	Susan Napier	
VIKING MAGIC	Angela Wells	
DECEPTIVE PASSION	Sophie Weston	
LOVE ON LOAN	Natalie Fox	
EDGE OF WILDNESS	Christine Greig	
LEARNING TO LOVE	Rosemary Hammond	
PASSIONATE ADVENTURE	Karen van der Zee	
THE BECKONING FLAME	Jessica Hart	
TOO SCARED TO LOVE	Cathy Williams	
NO GOING BACK	Stephanie Howard	
PORTRAIT OF CLEO	Joanna Mansell	
BAY OF RAINBOWS	Dana James	
A WARNING OF MAGIC	Kate Kingston	

If you would like to order these books in addition to your regular subscription from Mills & Boon Reader Service please send £1.70 per title to: Mills & Boon Reader Service, Freepost, P.O. Box 236, Croydon, Surrey, CR9 9EL, quote your Subscriber No:.................................. (If applicable) and complete the name and address details below. Alternatively, these books are available from many local Newsagents including W.H.Smith, J.Menzies, Martins and other paperback stockists from 9th April 1993.

Name:...

Address:...

....Post Code:................................

To Retailer: If you would like to stock M&B books please contact your regular book/magazine wholesaler for details.

You may be mailed with offers from other reputable companies as a result of this application. If you would rather not take advantage of these opportunities please tick box ☐